'JAN 1984

D1575212

This book may be kept

MOTH-KIN MAGIC

MOTH-KIN

Kathy

ILLUSTRATED BY

A Margaret K. McElderry Book /

MAGIC

Kennedy Tapp

MICHELE CHESSARE

Atheneum / 1983 / New York

For Kevin, Kristopher, and Katrina

Library of Congress Cataloging in Publication Data

Tapp, Kathy Kennedy.
"Moth-kin magic"
"A Margaret K. McElderry book."
Summary: Several members of a Mothkin family,
tiny people less an inch tall, must escape or
die when they are inadvertently captured by giants
and imprisoned in glass bottles used to study
plant life.
[1. Size and shape—Fiction.   2. Fantasy]
I. Chessare, Michele, ill.   II. Title.
PZ7.T1646Mo   1983   [Fic]   83-2782
ISBN 0-689-50288-5

Text copyright © 1983 by Kathy Kennedy Tapp
Illustrations copyright © 1983 by Michele Chessare
All rights reserved
Published simultaneously in Canada by McClelland & Stewart, Ltd.
Composition by Westchester Book Composition, Inc.
Yorktown Heights, New York
Printed and bound by Fairfield Graphics
Fairfield, Pennsylvania
Designed by Felicia Bond
First Edition

PROPERTY OF THE
NORTON PUBLIC LIBRARY
25176

CONTENTS

The Invasion

Like a great sleeping animal, the river had stretched itself in the spring sun, shaken the ice from its back, and woken up. Moving lazily at first, then with growing force, it foamed over rocks and logs. But it could not reach the very small shelters hidden in a cove high up on its bank.

Ripple lay on her stomach on a mossy ridge of that cove. From her high perch, she could see the people of her colony working at their jobs. The fishermen were dragging their nets down to the water. Fishing was urgent business in spring, when the baby fingerlings were still small. Very soon, these fish would outgrow both the nets and the fishermen's strength. By then the colony needed to have its whole year's supply caught and ready for drying.

Close by, a group of young children was playing a hiding game in one of the bigger cones. Ripple knew that game well. The many layers of the woody pine cones made perfect hiding places. But this time of year the leftover cones were rotting and dangerously soft. She was not surprised to hear one of the mothers calling the children away from the game.

Ripple pried a small pebble from the ridge and

dropped it in the water far below. She knew she should go and join the others. But she wanted to stay here for just a few minutes more.

The sun, the water, the whole river sang of spring. And today was the best day of spring, the day that Ripple had waited for so long. The day of the Gathering.

Excitement spread through her like a swelling bubble, ready to burst. Last year she had been too young to attend the Gathering. But tonight she would join the others of the colony in the clearing. There under the weeping trees, Uncle Kane, the storyteller, would tell the great legends of heroes and giants and of the coming of the magic.

The magic. Ripple drew in a quick breath. That was what she yearned most to know about. She had seen the older ones transformed by the magic in past seasons. This year she had finally reached her third cycle. At last she was old enough for the magic to come to her, too. Now she would be allowed to sit with the older ones at the Gathering.

She bounced a little on the ledge and threw another pebble. The excitement was almost unbearable. What wonderful new things would she learn tonight? Would Uncle tell why the magic came each year? Would he tell how it felt? Would he explain about the mysterious giants and tell the stories of her peoples' history?

She had waited so long for this day of learning. Now she had to wait still longer, until nightfall.

Mother and Uncle Kane approached, climbing the slope slowly, at Uncle's pace.

"There's my wanderer," Mother said loudly. Then, as they drew nearer, "Ripple, come down. Uncle and I have been looking for you. There's work to be done before the Gathering tonight."

Work. Always work. Ripple sighed. She knew what the next words would be even before Mother spoke them. "We must pull our share of the load, remember."

Ever since Father's fatal accident with one of the terrifying many-legged water creatures last fall, Mother thought only of "pulling our share" and of chores. Chores for herself, chores for Ripple. Netting, stitching, weaving, seed gathering.

The chores were always nearby. Ripple was sure that was part of the plan, to keep her safe at home, away from the mysterious moss-hung trails, from the leaping river, from danger...

"Mother, it's the warmest day yet, and there's plenty of time left—"

Mother glanced down at the water that had taken hold of the sun's sparkles. For a moment, her face almost let go of its worn-out look. She almost let the sunlight take hold of her, too. For that moment, she looked younger, prettier again. "It *is* warm—"

"Plenty of time later to watch the river," Uncle Kane said, puffing a little from the climb. He adjusted the tunic that just barely stretched over his very round middle, and caught his breath.

"Your mother is right, girl. There is much work to be done. We must prepare for this night of ceremony, of the telling of the great tales on the bank of the roaring river."

Mother took him by the arm. "Here, Uncle, sit down. You're tired after that climb."

But he shook his head. "I only came up here to help you find young Ripple. I must be on hand for the preparations! Come, Fern."

Mother motioned for Ripple to follow, as she started slowly down the slope with Uncle still puffing, still talking: "This is a day of days! Never has the sky been such a bright blue or the water so crystal clear . . ."

Ripple grinned. Uncle loved to talk. His voice went on and on, like the river running over rocks. When he was happy, as he was today, beautiful words tumbled out in a never-ending stream. When he was upset, it was best to get far away from the angry torrent. Tonight, at the Gathering, would be his moment of glory.

Ripple dropped one last pebble into the river.

"Plenty of time later to watch the river," she intoned in her deep Uncle Kane voice, but softly, so they wouldn't hear her. She ran her fingers through her short hair, trying to make it as bushy as Uncle's white mane, and strutted forward, stomach pushed way out. "A day of ceremony, of the telling of the great tales—"

Not bad. Not bad at all. Uncle was easy to do.

But she shouldn't poke fun. Uncle Kane was an elder. And people said that when he got deep into a story, his words came alive with a power of their own, and his voice held a force that could make the river turn around. She shivered, thinking about it. After tonight she would know if it was true.

"Ripple!" Mother called sharply.

"Coming." She slid off her rock, into the high spongy mosses.

Then all at once she was aware of a strange, loud rumbling, further up the riverbank. Like thunder, the noise filled the sky, shook the ground. Alarmed, Ripple hurried through the moss toward her mother and Uncle Kane.

The rumbling became an ear-splitting noise overhead. Ripple's eyes grew wide with horror, as she glimpsed huge beings crashing down the riverbank, blocking the sunlight, trampling the high grasses.

"Mother!" Ripple cried in terror, above the terrible noises. Then she dove down into the thick sheltering moss. She pressed her body as close to the earth as possible.

Mother slid toward her. Her arm went around Ripple tightly. "Stay down! Whatever you do, *don't get up!*"

"What—what is it?" Ripple could hardly speak the words.

"The giants," Mother hissed into Ripple's ear.

"Now I have seen them with my own eyes!" She was trembling. "So many of them!"

Then the clump of ground beneath Ripple was suddenly yanked upward. The moss patch tore loose with a violent lurch, pulling her away from Mother, from Uncle Kane. She couldn't yell; she couldn't even move. She was frozen to her dizzily swaying clump of moss and dirt.

The big open mouth of a huge bag swung toward her. She was heaved into the bag. The bag shut, and darkness closed around her like the night.

_____**II**

Prisoners

Ripple had no idea how long she stayed in that suffocating dark place. She was aware of movements, of jolts and jerks. She couldn't see anything, but she could feel the movements of the giant beings that had captured her. After a long while, the jerky movements stopped. The bag was slammed down with a painful thud. The loud giant noises drifted away, leaving a silence more frightening than the noise. A dead silence, with no splashes of river water, no whispering of wind, no buzzing and humming of river creatures.

All her life, Ripple had known the presence of the river. Even in winter, when the colony was in deep underground chambers and the river packed with ice, she could always feel the river's closeness. Where had the river gone? Or where had she been taken, that the river couldn't follow?

No water, no sun, and only her hungry stomach to mark the passing of time. A lot of time. But she didn't want to eat. She didn't want to do anything but stay pressed down against the dirt. Perhaps if she stayed there long enough, the terrible nightmare would end.

"Ripple? Ripple?" It was Mother's voice, searching, anxious. Ripple blinked. Her heart started pounding. She opened her mouth to answer, but only a raspy croak came out of her dry throat.

"Fern, she must be here. She was on the slope when *they* came."

Uncle Kane! Ripple tried again—pushed the words out.

"Mother! Uncle!" She stumbled forward as she saw two shadows coming toward her. Then Mother grabbed her out of the darkness, fiercely.

"You are here!" Her usually calm voice was wild-edged.

"What—what's happened to us, Mother?" Ripple grabbed her like a small child.

"We have been captured," Uncle Kane answered. His voice sounded as if someone had let the air out of it. He sagged back against the dark moss with a moan. "We are prisoners. Prisoners of the giants. What is to become of us?"

Ripple's heart jumped around crazily. Captives! Of the horrible giant beings of the stories and legends! But—

"Ripple, it's hard for you to understand," Mother said. "You don't know the stories yet, the stories of our people, Micarus. We are so few, in a world filled with these creatures. They have forms like us, it is said: arms, legs, faces, hands; but they are *huge*. Except during the time of the magic, we have always stayed in our cove, hidden from the giants' eyes. You would have learned all this at the Gathering. . . ."

Uncle Kane's voice rose above hers, full of misery. "Snatched from our homeland, tossed into darkness; the day of the giants has come again. We are cursed!"

Ripple wanted to cover her ears to block out his words, block out this dark place, block out the fear. "Mother, where are the others? Are they hidden somewhere in the darkness too?"

"No. We were the only three on the slope. I hope—" Mother swallowed, started again. "I hope they had time to escape."

"Then we are alone." The awful words slipped out of her mouth before she could stop them. Alone in the darkness. Their homeland smashed. Would those who survived the invasion be moving farther downriver, regrouping, starting over? If any of them *did* survive. If they had the strength to run fast enough—

Two shadows that were Uncle Kane's arms were waving about in the dark. He muttered, "This cannot be happening, not now, not here. The tales of giants' invasions are from such long ago times. In the days of Nimrod and Mellissa. . . ."

He was speaking of the old heroes, the old legends that Ripple had wanted so much to learn. But now she was dazed, blank. She couldn't concentrate on Uncle's words. After a while, his deep voice grew fainter. Ripple drifted into a sleep haunted with huge monsters.

At a great clamoring sound, Ripple's eyes flew open. The giants had returned to fill the world with their noise.

There was sudden motion. The bag opened. Light flooded in. Light everywhere, blinding her with sudden brightness.

"Steady, steady," came her mother's voice close to her ear. Ripple pressed against the concealing moss and tried to stop shaking.

Prisoners. Captives. In a world filled with huge monsters. Of course she had known about the giants, vaguely. All of the children of the colony had heard mention of the great scary creatures who lived somewhere in the world outside the colony.

Before his accident last summer, her own father and several other scouts had reported glimpsing a giant's form along the far banks. But even then, Ripple had felt safe from such dangerous creatures. The giants lived far away in the distance, far from her colony, her cove, her world.

But now there was no colony. No cove. No Gathering. Here, she would not even live long enough to learn about the magic—

No, she told herself firmly. Don't think of such things. And she forced herself to watch the giants' activities. Her eyes were used to the light now. Through the spongy thick strands of moss, she could see the vast figures of the giants and many strange objects. There were other clumps of moss, too, and plants.

"What are they going to do to us?" she whispered, grabbing her mother's arm.

"I don't know. Stay down. Don't let them see you."

Uncle Kane pressed close to the earth. The words that he muttered into the moss were ones that could not be repeated.

Another lurch. Before she closed her eyes against the sickening feeling, Ripple saw with horror the soft flesh of the giant's hand curved around the moss, as she herself might hold a tiny pebble— moving them toward a big container.

They were being squeezed through a tight place. Ripple could hardly breathe for the pressure. The pushing grew harder. The moss closed in around her. She struggled frantically for air.

They slid through the tightness, and the pressure eased. The next instant they were falling with their clump of dirt and moss. Soft, loose dirt broke their fall. But other things dropped all around them. This strange world into which they had been pushed was raining plants and dirt and rocks. One clump of dirt landed dangerously close. As she shrank away from it, Ripple saw a long stick reach down to shove it aside.

Another moss clump landed. Then a plant, some dirt, and more moss. This clump had a tall plant attached. The menacing stick jabbed at the plant, making it stand tall. Then the stick withdrew. The fall of dirt and debris ended.

Through the eerie silence of this new land, Ripple heard soft moans nearby.

III

The Silent Forest

Pushing under the trailing vines, Ripple and Mother crept to where Uncle lay twisted on the moss.

"My leg, my leg," he groaned. "There is a sharp pain in my knee. These old bones are brittle—"

"Lie still," Mother commanded. "And Ripple, you stay under cover, too." Her eyes darted nervously around the too-silent forest. "More things could yet fall on us."

But the rainfall of dirt and plants was evidently over. The noise that surrounded the giants' presence was gone, too. The three of them were alone.

From her vine plant camouflage, Ripple watched Mother examine Uncle Kane.

"Oooh!" he cried, jerking away. "Don't press there, woman! For the love of Nimrod, you must be more careful!"

Mother sighed. "It's a sprain, I think." She leaned back for a moment; her face wore a lost, frightened look. Ripple knew the same kind of look was on her own face. But Mother shook her head, as if to drive away the feeling, and turned back to Uncle.

"It will mend. But you must be careful. Let us do your walking for you for a while. And then we'll get you a walking stick—"

"It is useless," Uncle Kane whispered. "All is lost, don't you see? The time of the giants has returned." He raised his arms to gesture, but they flailed limply. Uncle was a pitiful sight, not at all his usual dignified self. His already overstretched tunic was ripped halfway up; his face and arms were smudged and bruised and scratched; his deep voice cracked as he hissed, "We are doomed."

Mother kept talking, half to herself. "We will make your bed here, under the shelter bush. We can prop the leg somehow. Help me, Ripple. There." She pulled Ripple aside, speaking in a low voice. "Your uncle is not young anymore. We must try to keep him comfortable, ease the shock for him. He's dazed by all this."

Ripple bit her lip. She was dazed, too, and hungry and miserable. "But Mother, what's going to happen to us? What *is* this place?" The tears were very close to spilling over. She gulped them back. She wanted to be comforted too. She wanted the splashing river water and her people and her home, not this dreadful forest prison.

"I—don't—know—where—we—are," Mother said, spacing each word carefully. "None of the old legends tell of a place such as this." And the scared, lost look flashed across her face again. But only for a moment. Then she straightened; set her jaw. "We'll—we'll find out. We'll plan. We'll watch. If we keep our wits about us, we can do it." She was talking to herself, really. "One thing at a time. First—we must find food." She looked past Ripple, to the silent forest beyond. "Out there."

Out there. That meant leaving the familiar clump of moss, their last link with home, and going into those shadowy places.

Searching out food in unknown territory had always been the job of the bravest and strongest of the colony. The scouts. Some of them, like her own father, never came back from their dangerous expeditions.

Ripple peered through the vines. Her heart was pounding all the way up to her head. But the tingling, scared-excited feeling was not all unpleasant. On the riverbank Mother had held her back from the trails, safe at home with safe chores. Not now. *We* must find food.

"Yes." Ripple spoke the word loudly, to drown out the rapid pounding of her heart. She stood straighter, head high. She was the daughter of a brave scout. "We must find food."

"This is a strange land. Any manner of creature could be lurking beyond the vines," Uncle warned, looking hard at Mother. She held up a hand, as if to stop his words.

"We will be careful, Uncle. Rest here. I hope we can bring back food."

"I . . . will . . . be fine." His voice had the tiniest hint of a quaver. "Go slowly. Step quietly."

They started across the flattened tangle of moss. Clumps of it lay strewn about haphazardly, not at all like the smooth velvety carpet that covered the riverbank. The plants, too, had a lopsided, uneven look, as if they were also out of place here.

"Careful, go slowly," Mother cautioned half a

dozen times during the first few tense minutes. But after they passed several plants without meeting any danger, they moved a little faster. Ripple's every sense was alert and quivering to the smells and sights of these woods. The uncertain moment each time of crossing into a new area gave her that tingly scared-excited feeling all over. It left her both tired and strangely eager for more.

Beyond the second vine plant they had their first stroke of luck. Nearly hidden in a moss clump was a half-torn mushroom. The sight made Ripple's stomach lurch with hunger. She took several ravenous bites before calling Mother. Nothing had ever tasted so good.

"The rest we can bring back for Uncle Kane," Mother decided, after they had almost satisfied their hunger. "I have my belt pouch to carry it in. But this is only one meal. We must search out a lasting source of food."

They checked by smell and touch each plant they passed: the tall treelike plant that shot great spikes toward the sky, the trailing vine with round, bright green leaves, a beautiful crooked bush covered with tiny white flowers, and a huge, velvety purple plant.

"Beautiful, but not edible," was Mother's grim comment after passing each plant. "We must look farther."

They turned away from the velvety plant, and

Ripple walked right into something hard and invisible. Her whole body reeled from the impact.

"Mother! There's something here. A wall or something!"

The substance that she had hit was very hard and smooth and as transparent as the river on a calm day. Pressing her face against the wall's cold smoothness, Ripple gazed out at the land outside the wall—a land where giant forms moved in the distance. Crouching lower in the moss, she trailed the wall for several steps. She could not find any break in the barrier. The clear wall continued for as far as she could see in both directions and higher than she could possibly reach.

"It's everywhere," she whispered. "It doesn't end at all."

Mother felt the wall, too. Touched, pressed, pushed, walked ahead, trailing the smoothness, and came back. She spoke in a low voice, more to herself than to Ripple. "There was that horrible fall. Afterward, the giants' voices sounded farther away. Everything was quieter." She gazed upward. Following her glance, Ripple suddenly saw for the first time that the sky of this forest was not a true sky at all, but was made of the same clear strong smooth material as the wall. It sloped above them, a clear dome. Squinting hard, she thought she could see an opening far far above them. And she suddenly understood.

"The giants are outside of this forest. And we are inside. This wall, or whatever it is, separates us."

"We fell through there," Mother said slowly, pointing to the tiny opening. Ripple shuddered. It was a long long way to the ground from that height.

Things began to make sense. "The plants and moss and dirt came through the hole, too," she said. "The giants put us here and the plants, too. It's not a real place at all, like the riverbank. It's a made place." But she didn't dare ask the next question. Why? Why had the giants made this silent forest prison? Ripple felt a sudden chill. "Let's go back."

"Yes." Mother glanced around nervously. "It is getting dark. And Uncle Kane will worry."

They had come a long way in their exploring; the shadows of evening were beginning to darken the quiet woods. At home, Ripple had always welcomed the coming of night, when so many of the river creatures awoke to fill the air with their sounds. Then she and the other children would gather at the water's edge to swim and climb among the vines. If she were there now, she would be running and laughing and talking with the others about the magic: when it would come to them, and how it would feel. She clenched her fists and pushed ahead.

Nighttime here was empty. No cool wind blew.

No creatures moved. The darkness was a smothering blanket.

"Stay close beside me, Ripple," Mother said. "We have only seen part of this land. We don't know what else is here."

They retraced their path through the wobbly, lopsided plants. Long before they reached their own familiar moss clump, Ripple began to feel the effects of the endless, nerve-shattering day. Each step became more of an effort.

Uncle Kane's face filled with relief when he saw them coming. "Ah, Fern, Ripple, you are a welcome sight," he called softly. They sagged down beside him on the moss. He sighed. "This is a lonely outpost. And you were gone far too long. I felt quite helpless and alone—but what have you brought back?" His eyes lit up at the sight of the mushroom bits bulging from Mother's pouch. He reached greedily for the food.

"Wonderful. Delicious," he said between noisy bites. "I thought I would never be able to eat again. But food speeds the healing. I need to regain my strength. Have you any more, Fern?"

Mother shook her head. "No, Uncle, it was only part of a mushroom. Yanked up with the moss, I suppose." She stretched out under the shelter vines. Her eyes shut; she looked already half-asleep. But she was still checking off tasks out loud. "We will look again, in the morning.

Strengthen our shelter. Learn more about that wall—"

Ripple's eyes itched with tiredness. Her body felt as heavy as a sodden log. But she couldn't relax and let sleep come yet. Someone needed to keep watch while Mother rested and Uncle Kane dozed off and on. She resolved to stay awake, to listen, to be ready for any night surprises in this eerie forest.

The next thing she knew, Mother was stirring beside her, and the forest shone with the dim light of early morning.

IV

The Intruders

The giants returned with the daylight. They filled the land outside the forest wall with noise and shadows. Mother and Ripple moved Uncle Kane to a deeper, more concealed shelter with a soft mossy ridge to support his back.

"Our first strategy is to stay completely out of the giants' sight," Mother told Ripple firmly. "The less they know of us, the better. It is possible that they don't even know how many captives they have." Mother had wiped much of the dirt from her tunic, smoothed the torn places, pulled her long hair back with a length of vine. Her eyes were dark-tired, and her mouth was very far from a smile, but her determined voice was comforting.

"Quite right. Quite right." Uncle Kane nodded. This morning his color was better. He looked more energetic propped against the moss instead of slumping dismally on the ground. And so far Ripple had not heard him mention "doomed" or "cursed" again. Perhaps he was feeling well enough to answer the terrible question she had to ask.

She glanced at him sideways, several times, before finally gathering courage to begin.

"Uncle," she started, crumpling a leaf strand in her palm. "Uncle—" and she plunged ahead. "Who are these giant creatures? Why have they captured us? What do they do to people? You know the old legends and stories better than anyone. You can tell me." She threw the crushed leaf bits to the ground. There, she had said it. Now she would have to listen to the awful answer.

"The giants—" Uncle began loudly; then he gazed out beyond the vines, where the real giants moved, and he dropped his voice.

"Vile, hulking creatures," he hissed. He tried to straighten his grimy tunic and sit straighter. "In the old days, the dangerous times before the founding of our river colony, much more was known of their ways. Those were the days of heroes and legend. When I was a boy, Old Elijah, the oldest of the storytellers, was said to know the most about the giants." Uncle shook his head. "Elijah, the dreamer. Some of his stories were preposterous, unbelievable. He claimed that once our people could even *understand* the giants." Uncle made a disgusted sound that came out a muffled snort. "Old Elijah spent too much time in his dreams. He forgot what was real. He even claimed that those long-ago giants had a name for us that lik-

ened us to the summer creatures of the air. Moth-Kin.

"Scum-rot, I say. Pure scum-rot. We are the Micarus people. We have honored our true name down through our history, just as we have honored the true heroes. Their stories of bravery are the *real* legends, the ones told at the Gathering." He leaned back against the moss, eyes closed. The long speech had tired him. "Ah, and here we are, too, snared by giants. . . ."

"You rest now, Uncle." Mother beckoned to Ripple. "We must search again for food. We will be back as soon as we can."

"And if you should find some more of those mushroom bits—" Uncle called after her hopefully.

With a sigh, Ripple followed Mother into the forest. Despite Uncle's outburst, she knew little more of the giant creatures than before. Uncle had gotten sidetracked with Old Elijah and forgotten her question. Hulking. Vile. Perhaps it was better not to know.

Still—she had caught a glimpse of something else. Something that excited her mind. Micarus. Moth-Kin. Real or not, it was a proud name. And beautiful. It hinted of the magic—

A few moments later they reached the clear wall that marked the edge of the forest. Blurred figures of giants and other huge objects could be seen on the other side of the invisible wall. When Mother tapped it softly, it made a clear, ringing noise.

"We have found this wall on both sides of the forest. It stretches up higher than we can see," she said grimly. "It is everywhere. There is no way out."

A huge shadow passed by, and they both ducked into a nearby vine. Ripple shuddered. Of course the giants could see through the wall, too, from their side. She crouched even lower. Vile, hulking creatures.

They crept away from the wall, toward a place where the forest sloped down gently. Halfway down the slope were some rocks and a small clump of bushes and trailing vines.

"Ripple!" For the first time there was excitement in Mother's voice. "If that plant is what I think it is . . . we must go down and see it closer."

The bright green leaves struck Ripple as familiar, too. Had she seen this plant somewhere along the riverbank?

Mother touched and sniffed the bush. "Yes! It is the one. Our people have used this for food. It was not first choice along the river, where we had so many food plants. But here I am so glad to see it!" She plucked a leaf and held it almost reverently. "There is water stored inside, too. And we need the water. There is no river here—"

The river. Ripple buried her face in the plant and tried to stop the memory of the wind and the

grasses and the soft clay ground and the warm
sunshine. She and Mother and Uncle Kane were
here now. And they had to survive.

She bit off a piece of the leaf. It was moist and
juicy as Mother promised, but it tasted slightly

sour. Still, it was food and water. "We can bring some back to Uncle. He'll be happy to know—" She stopped. Her body stiffened. She had seen a movement just now at the bottom of the slope, a sharp quick movement. The leaves of the bush still trembled slightly. And there was a darker form crouched behind it.

They were not alone in this forest.

V

Discovered

Uncle Kane's eyes opened wide with shock and surprise when Mother told him the news. "Who? Where?" He peered into the vines as if he half-expected to see the intruders standing there. "Someone like us? Are you sure? What did he look like? Did he see you?"

Mother handed him some of the leaves they had gathered. Her face pulled together in a frown. "We didn't get a good look, just saw the movement, the shadow. But there was someone."

"Mother," Ripple protested for the third time. "I *saw* whoever it was when he ran back into the vines. He looked like us. He's small. Why should we hide?" Glimpsing that lithe figure running into the forest had given her a surge of excitement and curiosity. For one quick moment she had almost run after him, crying, "You are not alone! We are here, too!" But Mother had grabbed her, pulled her back quickly into the bushes. And here was Mother again, shaking her head.

"Ripple, listen to me," she began wearily. "Think. If this person was another captured member of our own colony, would he have slunk away from us? Back on the riverbank, if we had greeted every small creature we met with open arms and smiles, we would not have lived very long. Some small creatures have stingers. Some have teeth. Some have sharp claws. Remember?"

"But this was a person. Not a long-legged river creature."

"Now young Ripple, your mother is absolutely right," Uncle Kane said, crunching on his ration of leaves. He made a face and spat some out. "Fern, you certainly found the bitter ones. But that's beside the point." He turned again to Ripple. "We must wait and give this creature a chance to show himself." He pointed a finger at Ripple. "Bravery is not foolhardiness. Our wits are our protection. The heroes of old..."

"I have an idea," Mother cut in. She had been sitting, tapping absently on a rough plant stem. Now she spoke in her firm organizing voice. Ripple hadn't heard that tone since their capture. "We'll build a tunnel. We've been sleeping between moss and vines, where any creature could catch us unawares in our sleep. We must tunnel down, as our people always do in winter." She was looking straight at Ripple, but it was easy to see that her mind was already racing ahead, working on the details, planning. "Yes, we must do it. It's the only safe way."

"But Mother," Ripple cried in dismay. "Not a tunnel! Not now, when it is so warm, when the river is—"

The river. Why did she keep acting as if they were only a short jaunt away from the mighty water and would return very soon? Why couldn't she just accept the fact that they were sealed in this horrible silent place where it didn't matter what time of day or year it was, where one had to do unnatural things like building tunnels in spring?

"Ah, but Ripple, there lies the cleverness," Uncle cried, brandishing his leaf. "To do the unexpected, to outwit the forces against us. Giants outside, intruders inside. Very clever, Fern. If there are unknown creatures in this forest prison, we will be far more secure underground."

Mother looked at Ripple. "You and I have both had tunneling experience. We can do it."

"And I can keep watch while you work." Uncle Kane finished the last of his leaves and stretched back against the moss with a sigh. "If it weren't for these old bones..."

Watching Uncle, Ripple couldn't keep the corners of her mouth from twitching into a grin. Back on the riverbank, she would have pounced on this chance to "do" Uncle Kane. "Hmm. Er . . . hum," she would have said in a deep voice. Flex the leg. Wince. Lean back with a sigh. "Can't be much help, I'm afraid. Bad leg. If it weren't for these old bones. But I'll keep watch." Snore. Snore.

It would have made the others double up with laughter. No one else could "do" people as well as she did. But her talents were wasted here. This wasn't the river.

She took a deep breath. "All right," she muttered, kicking at the moss. "Show me where to start digging."

Just then a great clanging noise filled the forest. Ripple jumped at the sound, then crouched down, her hands over her ears, and waited. This was the third time today that the horrible noise had happened. At least this time it did not make her shake so with fright. She knew now that it would only last a few moments, and that soon after it the giants would start moving noisily in their land. She uncovered her ears as the clanging ended. Sure enough, there were rumblings of movement beyond the forest.

"We can dig right here under cover of these vines." Mother was already clearing an opening in the moss. "We'll be hidden, but close to Uncle if he should need help." She worked quickly, efficiently. Back at the colony, Mother had often taken charge of tunnel construction and repair in the fall. It was all part of "pulling our share." Mother was efficient. She got things done right.

Ripple hated tunneling. She hated digging into the stubborn clay with hands or crude tools. She hated the dirt and clay in her eyes, the terrible ache of tired muscles. She preferred any other task to tunneling.

But here, she soon discovered, tunneling was entirely different. The soil was loose and light. It moved easily. She learned after going a short way down that it also collapsed easily. She had to pack the dirt hard as she dug.

Chores. Scooping, packing, carrying. Always chores. Just like back at the colony. Safe, stay-at-home chores instead of following the unknown trails, meeting the strangers, the dangers.

She could not get that person out of her mind. She was certain that he did not have claws or stingers. He was a captive of the giants, like them. And she wanted to know more about him—where he was living, what he ate, what he knew of the giants.

Mother was being too careful. If someone could find this stranger and talk to him, make Mother meet him—then she would see that the captives had to work together against the giants.

The idea hit her with such force that she nearly tumbled over with her fistful of dirt. She looked from the darkness below to the silent forest that beckoned. Well, why not? Someone had to do it. Why not her? She was quick, and she knew her way in the forest as well as Mother. She could spy too.

After all, scouts had always ventured into strange places to find food and learn more about the land. Exploring was valuable. Learning about new places and people was not wrong.

A few scoopfuls of dirt later, she took a long breath and started on her plan. "We will need more food," she began hesitantly. Then, in a louder voice: "Uncle Kane can't walk yet and you're busy here. I'll gather the leaves. I can go quietly. No one will see me."

Mother straightened. "Ripple, there is someone else in this forest. You don't mean to go alone!"

"I can spy as well as anyone. And I am very quick. You know that." She could see Mother wavering. Mother hated to leave a project for other chores, once she got going. She gave Ripple a long look.

"You will take the same vine path? And come directly back?" It was as good as decided then.

"Yes. I'll be fine." And she started off quickly, before either of them could change their mind. Her heart raced, too, as she hurried through the moss. By the time she reached the slope, she was panting from nervousness and the run. In her excitement, she almost forgot to stop and pick leaves from the bright green bush. She plucked quickly, her eyes probing the foliage around her.

Clutching her fistful of leaves, she crept farther down the slope. This was new territory. She hadn't come this far with Mother. Her feet made no noise on the soft ground. She was so intent on her stealthy walk that she almost collided with a bright glossy figure hidden behind a round bush. She drew back with a little cry of alarm, then clapped her hand over her mouth. Her cry hung frozen in the quiet forest. Still nothing moved.

She stared, fascinated, at the figure. This creature was like nothing she had ever seen. It had the form of the huge birds of the air that she had often glimpsed flying high over the river. But its folded wings seemed frozen against its sides and its eyes stared vacantly ahead. Not even the smallest quiver of life rippled its beautiful body.

But it wasn't dead. If it were, it would be lying limp on the ground.

After a few more minutes of staring, Ripple took a cautious step toward the creature. Nothing happened. Feeling braver, she came even closer. Then, summoning all her courage, Ripple reached out her hand. The bird figure still did not move, even when she touched the shiny bright surface. Its glazed hardness was like the strong clear walls that surrounded the forest. Had this creature been put here by the giants to guard the forest, just as the walls had been made to imprison them?

It couldn't be. This bird creature could not guard anything. It could not even move. She touched the wings wistfully. The magic—

All of a sudden she had the uncomfortable feel-

ing of being watched. She spun around, her eyes darting quickly, nervously, from plant to plant. Not a leaf stirred.

Her heart pumped faster. Her arms and legs tingled. But the forest was quiet, as always. She must have been mistaken. Yet, when she turned again to the bird, she was sure that watching eyes were boring into her back. Panic rose inside her.

Perhaps she had been totally wrong, and Mother and Uncle Kane were right. Perhaps there were unfriendly creatures here; creatures with stingers, or claws, or pincers, creatures watching her right now—

Even the shiny bird looked suddenly cold and unfriendly, with the fixed gleam in its unblinking eye. Ripple started backing away from it slowly, forcing herself to move cautiously in this open area.

The concealing vines above the slope were but a short distance away. In a few minutes she would be safe; she would be under their protective cover. Then she could run back to her own camp. Just a few more steps—

The loud clanging sound jarred the ground, followed by the usual noises and vibrations in the giants' land. Ripple's eyes went automatically to the invisible wall, now partly clouded with the forest's moist air. What she saw froze her to the ground in terror.

A huge giant's face, nose flattened against the clear wall, peered into the forest, staring straight at her as she stood trembling and exposed on the slope.

VI

The Rescuers

She couldn't move. She couldn't do anything but stand there, while her legs wobbled and her breath grated harshly. Then, without warning, a figure slipped from the bush just a few paces away. An arm shot out and grabbed her, yanking her across the soft ground, into the vine cover.

Panting, shaking, Ripple stared up at the boy who had rescued her and the girl standing next to him. Their slim bodies were like those of her own people. But there was a wildness about them. Long, untrimmed hair; dirty, patched-together tunics. They were watching her, too. What did they want? Ripple was sure the wild banging of her heart was the loudest noise in the bushes.

"Th... thank you," she stammered. She forced herself to look through the vines toward the wall. But the dark shadow and huge eyes were gone. She shuddered again.

The boy leaned back, still staring. He was wiry-thin, with brown curly hair and eyes that never stopped moving, darting, watching. His face probably looked pleasant when he smiled, but right now his expression was somewhere between a puzzled frown and a scowl.

"Diy!" He threw up his arms and turned to the girl. "What do we do now? If the giant *did* see her—"

"Then they'll know we are here in their bottle forest," finished the girl. She was pretty, with large gray eyes and dark hair spreading out in tangled curls all over her head. "Calm down, will you, Crick?" she said in a low voice. "It had to happen sooner or later. We can't stay hidden all the time."

"We have to!" the boy, Crick, cried. "Face it, Dreamhead. You know this forest is just an experiment to those giants. And if they find out we're in here, they might do anything!" He spat out a leaf he'd been chewing. "Diy! Pan must be told. Lissa, you tend to her."

The girl tossed her head. "Go on then," she snapped.

Ripple looked from her to the boy who was slipping back into the vine paths. Then she looked again at the wall where the horrible eyes had been. Things had happened too fast. Her head buzzed. Who were these two with their ragged clothes and sharp tongues? Where did they come from? They looked about her own age, yet they spoke as if they understood something about this forest. What had the girl called it? A bottle forest?

The girl crossed the shelter. She moved with

quick grace. Her gray eyes searched Ripple's face in a frank stare.

"Are you all right now?"

Ripple swallowed hard. The shaking still wouldn't stop. She would never be all right again. But she wouldn't admit that to this confident girl.

"Yes. I'm all right. But it—that—it saw me. . . ."

"If we are lucky, the foggy bottle walls kept the giant from getting a good look at you." Lissa scowled. The scowl was a little like Crick's. "Beasts. That's what they are. But you are safe now. They can't see you here."

She hesitated, then went on: "We've been watching you—my brother and I. We saw you touch the bird statue. We wanted to know more about you before we showed ourselves. . . ." Impulsively she put her hands on Ripple's. "I was so glad to see you here, to know that we were not the only ones trapped in this place!"

Just then, with a faint rustling of leaves, two figures slipped into the shelter.

"Here she is, Pan" Crick said with a dramatic sweep of his arm. The man behind him looked about Mother's age. His tunic was all holes and patches and dangling strings. Another patch piece was wound around his head, pulling back his long tangled hair. But it was his eyes that drew Ripple's attention. They were a calm blue, like the river on a sunny day; knowing eyes staring out of a rugged face and surrounded by deep smile wrinkles. Only they weren't smiling now.

"By the Mighty One," he murmured with a slight frown. He stepped closer to Ripple. "To meet one of our kind here in this cursed place. Girl, how did you come to be here?"

With great effort, Ripple looked away from his powerful gaze. She glanced over at Crick and Lissa sitting side by side watching her. Should she tell? She knew nothing of these three with their ragged clothes and wild looks. But she would learn nothing from them if she didn't take the risk. "I was so glad to see you—to know that we were not the only ones trapped in this place." It was an offer of friendship. After all, Lissa felt as she did. And this man who looked as strong and rugged as any of the scouts at home, this man with the clear eyes could surely be trusted.

She took a deep breath and let the awful story spill out. The invasion, the dark bag, the long fall, Uncle Kane's injury, the search for food. Pan interrupted frequently, with questions about life on the riverbank and about Mother and Uncle Kane. Lissa was silent, listening with a dreamy, inward look.

"Diy!" Crick said, wide-eyed, when she finished. "A river colony, fishermen, scouts, hunters!" "Diy" seemed to be his own word and meant anything from a curse to a compliment. This time he sounded impressed.

Pan pulled what looked like a piece of grass

from his belt pouch. There was a tiny seed sprout at the end; he put that part in his mouth and let the rest of the stalk dangle from the corner of his lip. Ripple had never seen such a thing before. Anyone else would have looked sloppy, even comical with a stalk hanging out of his mouth. But it gave Pan a brooding, thoughtful look.

"We didn't come from a riverbank. Never been so lucky. I've spent my life surrounded by giants, you see. I know some of their talk, some of their ways. But I've no real home."

"Vagabonds. That's what we are," Crick added with a smug look. "We go where there is food. Sometimes right into the shelter places of the giants."

Pan continued, "Lissa and Crick have been with me since they were very young. Their own rock home was flooded and their parents killed in a thunderstorm a long time ago." He scowled. "This spring I chose a bad place to camp, too. Our dirt was scooped up for this bottle forest, just like your moss. And"—he bit down savagely on the grass stem and spat out the seed—"we were trapped in here."

"It's a terrible time to be prisoners inside a glass bottle." Crick kicked at the low moss with his foot. Crick was always moving: pacing, or fiddling with leaves and branches, or kicking at something. "Outside now, everything is warm and alive and noisy. And we are in here, where it is damp and still and dead." He shook his fist at the vast clear dome overhead. "If only there was a way out!"

Ripple's mind was spinning with new words and new ideas, trying to understand all the incredible things these three were telling her.

"You mean," she said at last, wonderingly, "the giants did not come to invade our colony at all? They didn't even know we were there? They just wanted the—the moss!"

Crick nodded. "That's right. And that's why it's so important that they don't see us."

Ripple looked away from his accusing glance. "We know nothing about these giants," she murmured. "Uncle Kane was the storyteller of our colony. He tells the history of our people. But the giants of his stories are all from long ago times." She turned to Pan. "If the giants didn't make this place as a prison for us, why did they make it and drop all the dirt and plants inside? What is it for?"

Pan snapped off a new stalk of grass, leaned back and stared up at the clear dome beyond the vines. "Their words are hard to hear through the glass. But I know some things. The giants only spend daytimes here—they go to other shelters before dark comes. I think they come to this place to sit and learn. This forest is something they learn about."

"I see," said Ripple. But she didn't, really. She couldn't picture the terrifying, stampeding giants as creatures who sat and listened and learned things, the way her people did at a Gathering. They were monsters who trampled plants and shook the ground. And the idea that there were places to live besides the riverbank stretched her mind almost to the breaking point. She couldn't grasp these new ideas. Not all at once. She needed time to think it over.

Lissa leaned far back on the moss so she was almost lying down. She twisted a piece of hair around her fingers. "Rushing river...weeping trees...moss everywhere...our own people. Legends...stories. I can almost think of how it would all look." There was hushed excitement and wonder in her voice and a dreamy, faraway look in her eyes. Then with startling suddenness she snapped out of her dreamy pose. "Ripple, I want to learn more about those legends! Crick and I do not even remember our parents. Pan has taught us how to survive. But I want to know about our past, our people," she finished eagerly.

"Uncle Kane could tell you about all that," Ripple cried. "I will talk to him about you. I'm sure he will share his stories with you."

But speaking of her uncle brought back the memory of him dozing under the shelter plant and of Mother working on the tunnel and the long, long time that had passed since she left to gather leaves. She looked back uneasily.

"I can't stay any longer. I will go back and tell Mother and Uncle Kane about you. Thank you again"—she looked at Crick—"for pulling me away from those eyes."

"Be careful this time." It was the same voice he had used when he told his sister "Face it, Dreamhead." He was too smug, too bossy.

Ripple tossed her head. She had never let the boys or girls of the colony bully her. A sudden mischievous impulse ran through her.

"Diy," she replied loftily, matching Crick's tone and shoulder-shrug perfectly. She looked back and had the satisfaction of seeing his mouth drop open in surprise and Pan's and Lissa's grinning faces.

Then she started back, crouching low to the ground, well away from the wall. Back to her shelter, to Mother and Uncle, back with a whole new picture of the world to share.

_____**VII**

The Warning

"You did—what!" Mother's voice was dangerously calm and low. Mother never screamed. The more upset she got, the quieter her voice became. Now she looked straight at Ripple and said very quietly, "Tell me that again, slowly." Under that cool stare,

Ripple's excitement changed slowly to nervous worry.

"I . . . I—" She cleared her throat. "I . . . you . . . were digging, and . . . so . . . I went to get the leaves for us. I . . . went a little farther down the slope—to see if I could find the one who was spying on us. Then"—each word was taking longer to come out—"on my way back, that clanging started. A . . . giant . . . came over and looked at me, through the glass—"

"Great Nimrod!" said Uncle Kane. Then, "Through the what?"

"The glass. You see, someone pulled me back into the vines. A boy. He was the one spying on us, Mother. He and his sister." Stumbling over her own words in her nervousness, she got the story out. Mother sat very still throughout the telling.

"So we're not alone in this horrible place after all, Mother," Ripple ended. "There are other captives, just like us. And they *understand* the giants! We can learn from them—" She stopped and looked from Mother to Uncle Kane. They did not share her excitement at all. Something was wrong.

"Gypsies," Mother said to Uncle in a low voice. Then she turned to Ripple. "We won't go rushing down the slope to make friends." Her tone was very firm and definite. "They are gypsies, Ripple. They told you so themselves. And I know all about gypsies. Stragglers like them came to our river colony several times. They were lazy. They would not help with the work. One pair even left with a sackful of our food supplies." She shook her head. "These people who come from unheard of places might look like us and talk like us, but they have no culture. They are not to be trusted."

"True. Very true." Uncle Kane nodded emphatically. His voice rose. "We are the Micarus People. We have a long heritage and traditions. Ours is the blood-line of Nimrod and Mellissa and their band of pioneers; of the first river settlers!"

Ripple just stared at them. This couldn't be her kind, pretty mother talking like this about people she had never even met. About keen-eyed Pan and Crick and Lissa, who moved so gracefully, proudly, like a heroine herself. Their clothes certainly were ragged and their hair untrimmed. But who could be otherwise in this place? And what did culture have to do with it?

"They aren't lazy," she replied, standing taller and looking straight at her mother. "They're smart. They know a lot about the giants. They can even understand their talk. They know more than we do."

Mother sighed. "You're young. It's hard for you to understand. We are so few. Outnumbered and outsized. We survive only by working hard, being careful. We will wait and watch these people and find out what they're really like. Now—" She stood and her tone dismissed further argument. "I still think we should finish the tunnel. It just needs to be widened a bit at the base."

Chores. Details. Holes in the ground. When there was a whole new world to learn about.

"And stay away from those gypsies," Uncle Kane added, pointing a finger at her. He shook his head. "Glass, is it? A bottle? Gypsies tell tales. Could be all scum-rot. Probably is." He turned to Mother. "We don't need gypsies to help us out of here. We need the magic. *That* will carry us out."

A loud clanging interrupted him. Ripple silently followed Mother into the freshly dug tunnel as the giants stomped about their land. She worked in sullen silence.

It was bad enough to have to live without wind and water and all the familiar smells and sounds and people of home. But this dark tunnel shut out even the sunlight. And now Mother was keeping her from her friends below the slope.

She kicked at the dirt resentfully. She wouldn't stay down here much longer. This tunnel in springtime was wrong, unnatural.

Mother glanced at her from time to time. Twice she tried to make conversation. "Ripple, if you had ever gone to a Gathering, if you had been able to learn of our history, to understand that we were a proud community, not a band of stragglers—"

"We're not there anymore," Ripple said. "We're here. And so are Pan and Crick and Lissa. The riverbank got squashed, remember?" Talk of the Gathering still gave her a sick hollow feeling deep in her stomach. She didn't like to think anymore about what could have happened to the others.

Mother's lips pressed together tightly and she turned away, too. But a moment later, she tried again. "Listen, Ripple, there is our colony and, we are told, other colonies scattered throughout the giants' land. I don't know where or how many. During the time of flight, when the magic comes, some venture too far from their homes. Some have accidents, some even get lost. Some just decide to explore the world beyond their colonies. These are the ones who become the stragglers, the gypsies. Their children grow up without knowledge or culture. That is what happened to those people you met below the slope."

Uncle Kane's voice echoed down through the tunnel.

"Fern! Ripple! Come up here quickly. A boy is here! He says—oh, you must come quickly!"

Crick! Ripple raced ahead of Mother up the sloping tunnel. How had he found their shelter? And why had he come?

Crick stood by the mouth of the tunnel, panting hard, while Uncle shot questions at him.

"How do you know this? Oh!" He pounded his

forehead. "When will this dreadful thing happen? Great Nimrod, what will we do?"

"What is it?" Ripple asked. "What's the matter!" Crick looked exhausted, as if he had sprinted the entire distance between the two shelters.

Behind her, Mother climbed out of the tunnel, alert and tense.

Crick's words stumbled out between raspy breaths. "Pan heard—" He took a deep breath and started again. "The giant *did* see you." His eyes were wide, wild. "They think we're bugs, Pan says. They will put poison in. Soon." That short message left him wheezing for breath. He sat down. "Diy, never ran so hard in my life. Had to warn you."

Ripple looked from Crick to her mother to Uncle Kane. The giant had seen her; something awful was going to happen. That much she understood. But...

"Poison," Mother echoed. She stood very still, her face suddenly drained of color. "Poison kills. Some animals have poison in their sting. Do the giants, too, have a poisonous sting?"

Crick stared at the round opening in the dome above them. He was breathing a little easier now. "The giants will put their poison in there, over the whole forest. It's not a sting." He got up slowly. "That's all I know. I have to get right back."

"Wait." Through the horror, an idea suddenly sprang into Ripple's head. "If that poison will be

over the whole forest, we'll all be safer underground. And we just finished digging our tunnel.
It's wide at the bottom. Go get Pan and Lissa and
bring them here. Your shelter bush won't be safe
enough." She turned to Mother, pleading. "They
should come underground with us."

Mother looked dazed. She didn't seem to have
even heard. For once she was not ready with plans,
details. "Giants, poison," she murmured. "This
nightmare grows worse and worse."

Uncle Kane rose with effort. "Ripple's right.
The tunnel is safest." He started for the opening.
"I will have to get down it somehow."

It was obvious that neither Mother nor Uncle
was going to be any help. Ripple knew she would
have to make things happen herself. "Hurry, get
the others," she urged Crick.

He pressed his hands to his face for a moment,
then nodded. "I'll be back as soon as I can."

VIII

Poisoned

Ripple breathed a long sigh of relief when Lissa and Crick and Pan finally appeared at the bottom of the tunnel. "Hurry, all of you, before the giants put in their poison!"

But with three extra people, the burrow was very crowded. Ripple watched Mother take in the newcomers' ragged clothes and long, tangled hair in one tight-lipped glance, then move closer to Uncle Kane. Uncle, too, wore a disapproving frown when he glanced at them, but mostly he watched the tunnel.

"The giants' evil power has grown much stronger since the days of our ancestors," he murmured, half to himself. "Now they have poison, like the hairy river creatures."

"Get it over with, giants!" Crick cried. He moved from his niche to another crowded corner, then back again; stretched out his legs, pulled his knees up to his chin and moved again.

"Be still, Crick," Pan said, putting up a hand.

He was crouched near the tunnel entrance, tense, watchful. "It's starting."

And then they all heard it. A huge foaming sound like the noise of the river when it shot jets of spray over rocks. The giants' voices grew louder, thundering down into the forest, even to the tunnel depths.

There was a long whoosh, then another swishing sound. Ripple wanted to plug her ears, to block out the ominous noises. But she sat there shivering, listening for what seemed like hours, until the noises finally faded away into silence.

"Finished," Pan said, then shot out his arm as Crick moved toward the tunnel. "Not yet. That poison's got to settle. I know that much about it."

"Can it . . . kill us?" Ripple heard her own voice asking the dreadful question.

Pan pulled one of the slender grass stalks from his pouch. His face looked hard and tough. "Takes more than sprays of giants' poison to do that," he said grimly.

"But it's over the whole forest. The whole forest." There was a brooding, wondering note to Lissa's voice, as if she couldn't believe the horror of it all.

"We'll stay down here. We'll wait it out. Outsmart them."

"How long?" Ripple asked Pan. Her voice sounded squeaky, scared.

"The night anyway."

"All night!" Crick groaned. "In this crowded, stuffy place! And then what? After the night, then what?"

Pan gave him a long look. "This isn't the first time we've been in danger! Danger's always been around us everywhere. Each kind takes a different scheme, a different kind of bravery. There's been worse times than this and we made it through."

Crick kicked the dirt. "None's been as bad as this."

"All right. Let me tell you a story then. About when I lived in a garden in back of the giants. One day when I was looking for food, some huge, leggy, antennae creatures jumped toward me. Before I could turn away, from the other direction came a giant, pushing a roaring thing across the high grass. There was no place to go. I was trapped. I thought, this is it. This is the end."

"What did you do?" Ripple and Crick asked together.

Pan grinned slightly. The smile made his eyes warm again. "The giant's leg passed right by. There wasn't thinking time." His grin widened. "I climbed the foot. There was material covering it. I hung on tight. Off went the foot, away from the stalking creatures. When that leg stopped, I got down quick and *ran!*"

Ripple could just picture Pan clutching onto a huge, stomping giant's leg. It was incredible, unbelievable, and somehow funny, too. Mother was watching Pan out of the corner of her eye. It was a curious, wary look, as if she was trying to figure out this gypsy who could ride giants' legs and live to tell of it.

Ripple felt a quick stab of triumph. Mother was being forced to get to know Pan and Crick and Lissa. She would see who was right.

Pan was watching Mother, too. "There's different kinds of danger. You keep your wits about you, hang onto your courage, ride them through—"

Crick stood, trying to juggle two dirt lumps in the air. "You outsmarted them that time, Pan!" One of his dirt clumps landed on Lissa's head. With a little cry, she jumped up and grabbed his hand.

"Outsmarted them. Outsmarted the giants." Uncle Kane spoke suddenly from his corner. "Yes. Yes!" His voice got louder; a strange glow lit his deep-set eyes. It gave his old wrinkled face, with its shock of white hair, a look of power and mystery. "That is it. That is the way the heroes of old survived. The legends tell of such bravery against the giants."

Lissa dropped Crick's hand. She crossed the small room and dropped down beside Uncle. "Those stories of the past," she said in a low, earnest voice. "Tell us."

It was hard to know if Uncle Kane even heard her. His eyes, burning like two flames, were in some faraway place. Ripple felt shivers run up and down her spine.

"In the days of our ancestors," he began slowly, in a hushed voice, "a large colony of our people was settled deep in the forest by a running stream. But giants invaded the forest, chopping down the great trees, banishing the animals and small creatures, and our people feared that they would perish.

"Nimrod, leader of the colony, offered to take an expedition across the dangerous giants' land in search of a new place to live. Only the bravehearted in the colony agreed to go with him. The others remained in the doomed forest; nothing was heard of them again.

"Nimrod and his mate Mellissa and the others had a difficult and dangerous trip through the giants' territory. They did not know the land. And giants were everywhere, felling trees, hunting game, trampling and scalping the land." As Uncle wove his tale, he sat up straighter; his voice grew deeper, stronger.

Ripple watched, entranced. Uncle was a different person. Not a bossy old man, not a whiny, hobbling invalid, but a storyteller with burning eyes and a rich voice. This was what happened at a Gathering. And her stomach gave a little lurch, as it always did when she thought of home. This was Uncle Kane's power as a storyteller that everyone talked about. He was taking them away from the poison and the crowded tunnel, to faraway places and faraway times.

"Nimrod and Melissa were the greatest of the heroes," Uncle continued. "They led the tired pioneers at last, not to another woods stream, but to a mighty river. They kept the rest going when they would have stopped and given up. They outsmarted the many hungry and savage creatures that would have killed them for food. They managed to avoid the giants. They found food. And the wonder of it all"—he dropped his voice—"is that they had to do it all in the spring, before the time of the magic had come. Their brave deeds were done without any help from summer's gift of flight."

There was silence for a long moment after he finished. Then Crick opened his mouth, and Ripple knew what the word would be before it came out. "Diy!" It was a cry of wonder.

Lissa hugged her knees up to her chin. "Wonderful brave people," she breathed. "To do all those brave things. Can you imagine? Our ancestors . . ." Her voice was hushed, dreamy.

"Watch out." Crick shook his head. "She's going into one of her moods." He was right. Lissa's eyes glowed with a faraway kind of rapture. She was still in the place of Uncle Kane's story.

A satisfied smile tugged at the corners of Uncle's mouth. "Ah, the magic, the gift of summer." He sighed. "I have fables to tell of that, too. Another time."

Mother had been sitting very straight and dignified, a little apart from the others. Now she spoke. "We need that magic now. With the power of flight, we could escape this horrible forest and somehow find our way back to our people." She looked up into the tunnel as she spoke. And Ripple's thoughts switched from the heroes of long ago to the awfulness of now. They couldn't stay in this hole in the ground forever. Sometime they would have to go back up, back to the poisoned forest.

"We can't wait for the magic," Crick blurted. "Who knows if the magic will even come to us here, where there is no weather and no sun and no wind. How can the magic find us here?"

"The magic will come." Lissa had snapped back from her daydream. She straightened and faced her brother. "Everything else is wrong here, but that *has* to come. Then we will have power, too. Then we will break free!"

IX

The Scent of Death

They spent a cramped, uncomfortable night. At first, Ripple tried to sleep, curled in a corner. But sleep would not come. Her mind was too full of fear, and the tunnel too crowded. After Crick bumped into her for the third time in his pacing, she gave up.

Lissa spoke for her. "Crick! Sit down, will you! There's no room to pace!"

"I can't!" he exploded. "I just can't!" And he turned to the wall and scratched big angry marks into the dirt.

Ripple sat up and pulled her knees to her chin. She caught Pan watching her.

"Hard to get comfortable, isn't it? Hard to sleep. I won't even be able to think straight when my lantan seeds run out." He frowned and spat out a seed. Out of the corner of her eye, Ripple saw Mother turn away with a look of disgust.

In the next few moments of quiet, Ripple tried again. Uncle had dozed off in his corner. So could she. She would *make* herself fall asleep to get through this awful night.

This time it was Lissa's voice that pulled her back; made her open her eyes.

"The giants dropped poison,
They want us dead.
Like heroes of old,
We'll survive instead."

There was a dramatic fierceness in her hushed voice. With her cloud of black hair and straight back, she could have passed for one of the old heroines herself in the shadowy dark tunnel. But Crick wasn't impressed.

"Another of your verses?" he scoffed. "You do all right with words and daydreams. But how's your throwing arm?" He tossed a pebble at the wall.

Lissa rose. With a haughty glare at Crick, she took one of the pebbles and threw it hard.

Ripple watched with a tiny half-smile. These two, brother and sister, were so different and so alike. Crick couldn't sit still for a minute; he had to be always moving. Lissa could withdraw for a long time into her moody, thinking place. Yet they were both quick, impulsive, deep-feeling. She liked them. Both of them.

"Here, you try, Ripple." Crick tossed her a pebble. Then, as she stared at him, "We'll go crazy if we don't *do* something."

Strangely, throwing that pebble made her feel better. And the game made time pass. When they tried bedding down again, sleep did come. And with it dreams.

It was winter in her dream. She was back in the cold-weather tunnel network along the riverbank. Then the earth grew warmer. She could hear the splashing of the river outside and the spring calls of the other creatures.

But something was wrong. She couldn't find the way out of the riverbank tunnel. She kept going and going. After a long while she was sure she was heading deeper into the earth instead of toward the outside. Panic rose inside her. She started running. Faster. Faster.

"Ripple, wake up." Mother's voice spoke in her ear. "It is very early. Pan says the giants do not come to their land until later in the day. So we are going aboveground now."

Aboveground. The word jolted Ripple from one nightmare to another. She jumped to her feet, instantly wide awake, and joined the others at the tunnel entrance.

There was a scared feeling in the air. Ripple could feel it all around her: in the way Mother's hands were clenched hard together, in Uncle's unusual silence, in Crick's grim, "Diy, let's get it over with," in the tight look on Pan's face.

Mother bent down to Uncle Kane. "We will

come back and help you above ground," she said. "Wait for us here."

Lissa joined Ripple. "The poison," she whispered, white-faced. "We have to face it now." She stood straighter then, made her voice firm. "The... the heroes of the old stories had to face dangers, too. And they made it through."

Ripple straightened. "It takes more than a giant's poison to get rid of us," she replied, trying to sound tough and sure, like Pan. But her breathing was quick. And her heart was pounding hard.

Lissa's hand reached for hers. It was easier going to meet the poison with someone else beside her. Someone whose hand was cold, too. Someone who stood straight and tall. Someone who was beginning to feel like a friend.

Before they even reached the surface, the strange evil smell wafted down to them. By the time Ripple climbed out of the tunnel onto the moss of the shelter, her throat and eyes and nose were burning from the sickening fumes, and her head ached. She had to fight the urge to turn and run, back into the cleaner air of the deep tunnel.

"I... feel... sick," Lissa said, hunching over. Mother knelt down, with her face in her hands.

"Ripple, stay here. Don't go any farther."

Pan pushed ahead slowly, as if every step was an effort.

"We can't live here!" Crick choked out. "We can't stay in this poisoned forest. We'll *die* here!"

Mother grabbed a branch stem for support and tried to stand up. "We must go back, at once."

Pan stumbled back, choking, coughing. He held out a fistful of the round green food leaves. "Wanted to check the food plant. The stuff . . . is . . . wet . . . on the leaves. Some of the . . . bottom ones . . . were dry."

At the bottom of the tunnel, Ripple crumpled on the dirt, dizzy and weak. The others sprawled around her, still coughing.

"By the Great Nimrod!" Uncle Kane cried. He hobbled over to Mother and touched her shoulder. "Has the poison done this?" His question came out like a moan. "Ah, then we are finished. The curse is upon us forever. . . ."

Pan slumped, head on knees, against the wall. At Uncle's words he sat up. He waved his leaves like a fist.

"If we have to, we'll wait this poison out. We'll live through it! We're strong." His voice was thick and slow, but there was something else in it, something stronger than the sickness. It made Ripple prop herself up and look at Pan, then at the others.

Crick's eyes were shut. Lissa was doubled up into a ball. Mother was watching Pan. Her eyes held a strange expression. Wonder? Surprise? Respect? But then dizziness swept over Ripple and she had to lie back.

For the rest of that day, it was hard to believe Pan's words that they were strong enough to survive. Ripple's legs felt as weak as crumbling earth, and her stomach refused the foul leaves, and her head spun. It was hard to think strong thoughts in the dark cramped tunnel.

"The final spell of the giants," Uncle murmured from his corner. He was the only one sitting now, the only one who had not breathed the poisoned air. "We need the magic to break through the spell!" The complaining sound left his voice, turned slowly into that other tone, the deep powerful voice of his storytelling. It ran like a shiver through Ripple, reached past the weakness and dizziness, as he began in a hushed whisper: "I will tell you the tale of *our* power, of how the magic came to us. Perhaps hearing it will give us new strength.

"In the beginning days, when the land was new, the Mighty One made the animals and gave them their homes. He made the giants and set them in their land. Then he made the Micarus people and gave them forests and streams to settle.

"Those were good times. The forest was full of berries and mushrooms and edible roots and juicy leaves. The huge plants gave protection and shelter from all the stalking creatures. The streams sparkled, the sun shone, and the giants stayed far away in their land, busy with their own affairs.

"But then things changed. The rains stopped. A drought came and parched the land. Many streams dried up. Rivers sank lower. Plants wilted and died. The ground grew hard and cracked. Food was scarce. Each day, the people had to travel farther and farther to find anything to eat. Hungry animals prowled constantly, all around them. Many of the scouts and food gatherers were killed. The people of the colony wondered if any of them would survive to see another year.

"At last Marco, the old weaver, set out to find the high mountain beyond the forest, where the Mighty One was said to live. He took his young apprentice, Julan. Together they traveled across the dry parched land. Some days they found nothing at all to eat. But Marco was determined to seek out the Mighty One and ask for his help, so he and Julan continued until they reached the high mountain. Together they climbed to the misty summit where the Mighty One was said to live.

"Old Marco was weak and ill by the time they reached the top. He did not make it back. Julan returned alone with the wondrous tale of that meeting with the Mighty One. And the whole colony gathered along the sluggish stream to hear his story.

"This is what Julan told. Marco met with the Mighty One. He told about the plight of their people and asked for help. Then the Mighty One praised Marco and Julan for their bravery. He said because of their perseverance and bravery he would send a gift to their people to help them find food and escape enemies in these hard times. He would put wings on their backs during the dry heat of summer, just like those of the buzzing creatures of the air. And when the cold weather came, and the time to tunnel underground, the wings would dry and wither and drop off—to grow again each year in summer's heat. And that," Uncle Kane ended solemnly, "is how the magic came to our people; how we came by our name Micarus and the gift of flight."

Ripple opened her eyes. She had only grasped part of the story, as her uncle's voice faded in and out through waves of dizziness. This was what she had yearned to hear at the Gathering: the tales of the old times and the magic. Such tales were meant to be told by the surging river, not in dark, dead tunnels. Even so, the power of the story was stronger than the sickness, stronger than the darkness. She shivered. Micarus. Moth-Kin. . . .

"Do you think it really happened like that?" she whispered to Lissa, who was lying beside her.

Crick rolled over with a groan. He held his head. "No, of course not," he snapped. "It's not true. It's just an old tale made up long ago when people didn't know any better. We have flight because that's the way our bodies are built, that's all. But it won't happen here, in this prison of the giants."

"It's a beautiful story." Lissa turned on him fiercely. "Think of the strength and courage of that old weaver! Think of him saving his people who were dying of hunger. Think of it!" Her voice shook a little. Ripple looked at her in surprise. Uncle had brought Lissa right up to the mountaintop with Julan and Marco.

Lissa gave Crick a haughty look. "Crick, you know less than those people of long ago. Don't make fun of the story."

Uncle's voice came in a powerful whisper from the other side of the tunnel. "It will come. The magic's been promised. It will free us."

The night passed like a bad dream, with fits of wakefulness between short, restless sleeps. Ripple wakened from one such sleep to a peculiar sound. The noise was soft, so soft that at first she wasn't sure that she had really heard it. She lay very still, listening hard. Then it came again: drip, drip, drip, on the forest floor above them. But how could such a sound be possible in this forest prison?

Moving quietly and quickly, so as not to disturb the others, she started up the tunnel. She wouldn't go far. If the poison air overcame her, she would go back down to the safety of the tunnel.

The dripping sound grew louder, more definite. And the smell in the air was less powerful. Her head was still clear when she reached the surface. She pushed aside the vines that covered the opening and crawled onto the dirt.

Her eyes opened wide. For a long moment she let the sight, the sound, and the feel of clear wetness surround her. Then she turned and ran back down the tunnel as fast as she could.

"Mother," she yelled. "Pan, Lissa, Crick, come quickly! It's raining!"

X

The Glistening Forest

They stood beneath the shelter vines and watched the cool drops of water fall to the ground, first slowly, then harder and faster.

"Rain," Lissa murmured, wide-eyed. Then louder, "Rain, everybody! *Rain!*" She almost shouted the words.

"Can it really be?" Ripple asked. "I mean, rain out of the sky, like we had back in our home?" She put out her hand and a piece of cool wetness splashed on it. "It feels like rain."

Pan cocked his head, staring up through the tangled vines, up toward the sky dome hole. "No real sky up there, just glass. Outside our forest is only the giants' shelter building." He shook his head. "Can't be rain. Only way we can get water is from the giants pouring it in, just like they put in the poison."

"Careful, then!" Mother pulled Ripple's arm. "You heard what Pan said. The giants are out there. Do you want to be seen again?" Her voice was sharp. Her face, usually so clean, was dirt-lined, with tired, dark puffs under her eyes. "Do you want them to know we survived their poison!"

The poison. Ripple frowned, took a sniff. Only faint traces of the awful fumes remained. But how— she looked around at the others. But Crick said it first.

"The rain got rid of the poison!" His face opened into a real grin. "Washed it right into the ground!" He punched Pan's shoulder lightly. "Right again, Pan. We will make it. The rain saved us!"

"Rainwater..." Lissa was smiling too, her moody, inward smile that held secret thoughts. "It made pools by our rock shelter back home, deep pools. Then the sun would sparkle on them. Gold, red, purple..."

Crick rolled his eyes, grabbed his sister by the shoulder. "Diy, Lissa. We're *here* now. Wake up. Look around, Dreamhead!"

Ripple was grinning now. And Pan. Mother reached out to touch a dripping leaf. "Rain," she said. And for the first time since the invasion, a real smile touched her face. The smile seemed to be directed at Pan, who was staring out past the shelter, into the glistening forest. Then, just as quickly, the smile was gone.

"The rain will clean the leaves. We will have food again," she said.

But a puzzling thought nagged at the back of Ripple's mind. "Why did the giants want to wash away the poison they just put in? They wanted to kill us. Did they change their minds?"

Pan bit down on his limp lantan weed. "I think these giants are young. They don't really know what they're doing. After our capture, we lay in that bag, listening. It was easier to hear then." He spat out the seed, and Mother winced. "Anyway, I heard more of their talk. This bottle forest is their experiment." He shrugged. "They might have just decided that the plants needed water, and it's our luck that they did."

Ripple turned at a sudden heavy clomping noise. Uncle had labored up the tunnel and stood behind them, puffing.

"Look, Uncle," Pan said, smiling. "What do you think?"

"Rain?" he said, looking around. Then louder, "Rain! Yes! It is right. It is so in the legends." He was still wheezing. He leaned against a branch and took a deep breath, as if to fill his lungs and voice with strength. "And the time of the spring rains came and the river roared with power." His voice swelled. "The pioneers saw the earth come alive. They felt new strength in themselves to reach their destinations." The silence that followed his words felt almost reverent.

"From the tale of the journeys of the first pioneers," he added. He sat down, tired again. "Ah, this old leg. Fern, you must help me back."

But his story had left a spell in the air, a spell that quivered like the sparkling drops all around them.

Ripple whispered, "I want to see the whole forest while it's like this." They had been cooped up in the dark tunnel for so long. And the forest looked suddenly inviting, an enchanted place where every leaf shimmered. Her muscles felt ready to explode.

Crick sprang up. "The bell just clanged. The giants have left. We won't have to stay hidden."

Lissa pressed a wet leaf against her face. "The time of the spring rains came," she echoed. "And the river roared with power." Her voice was soft, dramatic. "I can almost see it: the moving water, the blowing grasses, the shiny wet plants. Just like this forest." Suddenly she was the eager impulsive Lissa again. "Crick's right, for once. We should run through this forest of sparkles!"

"I don't know," Mother said slowly. "There's time now to plan. We should widen the tunnel, gather more leaves. We don't know what will happen next."

Ripple listened impatiently. Crick was already out of the shelter, with Lissa close behind him. Mother couldn't hold her back with chores this time! She looked to Pan. He nodded with a little half-grin, and waved her on. Ripple stared back in surprise. But only for an instant. Then, with an answering grin, she slipped quietly into the forest.

The moss felt light and springy. The leaves had a sheen to them. The forest seemed suddenly a glistening wonderland, not an evil prison of the giants.

Of course, nothing had changed. They were still in the bottle prison, still circled by glass, and still captives. But the forest was clean and sparkling wet, and that was all that mattered right now. That and the running, climbing, chasing, laughing. Crick was so fast he seemed to be everywhere at once. Ripple could hardly keep up with him. Lissa was quick, too, but even in running games, she moved with poise and grace.

When the noise and clanging announced the giants' return, the three of them left the vine paths and dived into a small shelter beneath the velvet bush.

Crick flopped down. "My legs feel better than they have since we got dropped in this place." He picked up a short branch. "I found a sharp pebble yesterday. If I use it on this branch, maybe"—he began rubbing—"I can shape a point. Make a spear—"

"For what?"

"To throw at the giants! Or to break the glass!" They all laughed at the impossible boast. "Or at least to practice my aim on a bush."

Ripple watched Crick work, head bent over his

lap. Crick's mind was like the rest of him, bouncing, jiggling, never still. Crick could make a game out of a tunnel wall and a pebble; he could see a spear in a branch. But he wasn't the only one with talent.

She put a long strand of moss in her mouth, let it dangle out of the corner, then stood with her hand on her hip, making a crunching noise with her teeth. "The way I see it," she said in a deep, thoughtful voice, "I'm about out of lantan weeds."

Crick clapped his hand over his mouth. The branch fell to the ground. And Lissa doubled up laughing.

"Oh, Ripple," she choked. "Where did you learn that?"

"I don't know." Encouraged, she grabbed a branch, stood with feet apart, and tightened her face with fierceness. Leaning back, she threw an imaginary weapon up toward the sky dome hole. "Diy, take that giants!" she cried. This time Lissa laughed till the tears came. And Crick pushed her over.

It was a magical afternoon. The raindrops had cast a spell on them as well as the forest. They ran, climbed, laughed, chased. An evening game brought them right up to the strange shiny bird, still staring straight ahead with empty eyes. Ripple's mood changed as she neared it. She was still wary of the stiff silent creature—a statue, Pan called it.

But Crick promptly ran up, threw an arm around the smooth neck, and hoisted himself onto the bird's shiny back. "I've wanted to do that ever since I first saw it," he called down.

Lissa touched the folded wings. "Wings," she murmured. "I wonder how they will feel?"

Ripple looked at her, startled. "I wonder about that, too," she said. Their eyes met. A knowing look. They both felt it then, that curious yearning and wonder about the magic.

"Pan says it's like an itch almost," Lissa said softly. "He says it builds inside you just before the wings start to form. Then there's new energy when the wings spread. Like a bud opening." Her voice dropped even lower. "In your colony, with all those other people around, did you see—"

Ripple shook her head. Her voice was low too. "I never saw it happen. I only saw the older ones come back after the change."

Lissa nodded. "It was like that with Pan, too. Each time the magic happened while he was away on some trip." She leaned back against the shiny bird and stared out across the forest. "I think he knew when it was time for it to happen. He left on purpose. We'll know too—when it is time."

"Yes," Ripple breathed. A shiver ran through her, speaking out loud of these secret wonderings. So Lissa and Crick were also in their third season cycle, the time of waiting for first magic.

Crick slid down. "It's getting late." He shoved his sister playfully toward the slope. Ripple knew he didn't like to talk of the magic. He didn't believe it would come here in the bottle prison.

The tiredness she felt in her muscles as she bedded down that night was a good tiredness, much better than the ache brought on by poison, or the cramped soreness of the nights in the tunnel.

But the enchantment was gone the next morning. The first thing she noticed when she awoke was the moist heaviness of the air. The whole forest was dank and misty. The glass wall was too steamy to see through. The moisture surrounded Ripple with a warm clamminess. She couldn't shake it off. It was everywhere.

"Rainwater never made the air so heavy in the river colony," Mother said, worried. "The water went into the ground; it never got so muggy as this, even before a thunderstorm."

With the glass so fogged up there was no need for caution. It would be impossible for the giants to see them. But Ripple didn't feel like starting up any games. The light, happy feeling of yesterday was gone. In its place was a steamy sogginess that made them all cross and sweaty and hot.

The next day the glass was still foggy; the air still wet and muggy. Ripple went that evening to pick leaves from the eating plant. She yanked several leaves from their stems. Then she leaned closer, frowning. There was something wrong with the bush. A fine web was forming on the leaves, coating them with fuzzy whiteness. She started to touch it, then drew back. There was something menacing about that white web.

She took several backward steps, still staring, then broke into a run, back toward the shelter.

XI

The Web

Mother stared at the fuzzy webbing. "Don't touch any of these whitish leaves," she ordered. "It could be—" and she took a deep breath and shut her eyes. "It could be another kind of poison."

Ripple stepped back even farther, remembering the sick, dizzy feeling. "But it's our food! What will we do! Will—will Uncle Kane know what it is?"

Mother started to speak, then hesitated. "Pan has lived so many places. He seems to know— quite a lot. Perhaps..."

"I'll go get him." Ripple started toward the slope quickly, on the hidden vine trails they had all come to know. Things were changing. Mother wanted Pan's advice. Pan was smart and brave. Mother knew that now.

They all came back with her. Pan squatted beside the bush. "By the Mighty One," he muttered.

"What is it?" Crick hovered beside Pan, sniffing, staring along with him.

Pan straightened, pushed back a lock of hair that had slipped from his ragged headband. "Strange, it reminds me of something, somewhere. I think—it was in a garden I lived in two springs ago. It was a very wet spring. And a gloomy, soggy garden. I saw this web stuff growing in log cracks."

Ripple glanced at the steamy wet glass wall that circled the forest, then at the shiny moist leaves of the nearby vine plant. A wet garden, Pan had said. So was this. What could be wetter than this bottle forest, where the very air was laden with water? Perhaps that was the reason for the rain after all; it was all part of the giants' diabolical scheme to poison the forest and contaminate the food supply.

"Will it . . . hurt us?" Lissa whispered, backing away from the plant as if it would uncurl and spring at her.

"I don't know." Pan plucked one of the still-healthy leaves on the far side of the bush. "So, from now on, we eat only this kind."

"While they're still left," added Crick bitterly.

Ripple whirled to face him. "Do you think this stuff could *spread?*" she asked, horrified. "What could we do for food then? We've explored the whole forest now, and we know there're no other plants we can eat."

"We're not starving yet," Pan said. He reached into his pouch and dangled a limp, straggly lantan weed before them. "Last one. And no crunch to it left. It's practically dripping." He threw it down. "Curse this place!"

A strange half-smile crossed Mother's face. Pan saw it, for he said, "Can't think right without my lantan!" Then, even more surprising, he began to grin, too. A sheepish sort of grin.

Ripple shook her head. Mother was hard to understand sometimes. But at least she was smiling. They all needed smiles now. Lantan weeds weren't the only things going. Tunics were shredding; pouches were ripped so they barely held anything. Mother's hair, which had always shone so at home, was matted and stringy. Ripple knew her own was no better. They were a ragged lot. And even the food supply was threatened now. Yes, they needed smiles.

"We'll watch the plant," Mother said. "And if necessary, we'll pick the healthy ones ahead. It's all we can do."

The white fuzz did grow. Like an evil plague, it began to wrap the whole side of the bush in its web. During the next few days, Mother plucked many of the leaves from the healthy side of the bush and stored them in the tunnel. Uncle Kane, his leg almost back to normal, walked slowly down the slope to examine the plant.

"Ah, we have the same wretched fortune as the first pioneers. Our trials were theirs, too." He intoned softly: "When the weary travelers finally reached the great river, they wanted to stop and settle right away. But Nimrod forbade them to stop there, for it was a dark, wet, drippy land where the sun hardly shone. It bred great mushrooms, and a whiteness covered many of the plants. A place of dampness and rot and death."

He sank against the bush. "I am an old man. Too old and weak for such troubles. Ripple, find me some good leaves. I need strength to help heal this leg."

But Ripple wasn't listening anymore. "Dampness and rot and death—" Those words hung over them like a prophesy of doom, as the fuzzy webbing gradually ensnared most of their food plant and reached out to cover the nearby moss. The healthy leaves were scarcer and duller. There were not enough to go around. Ripple felt hungry, even after a meal.

"If only the magic would come to us!" she cried to Crick and Lissa, as the three of them sat brooding in the vine shelter. With the glass gradually clearing, they had to take cover when the giants were present.

Crick broke a leaf from their bush and hurled it savagely to the ground. "Don't talk about the magic! The only kind of magic that can reach us here is the evil power of those giants." He glared up at the sky dome hole that taunted them always. "There *must* be some other way—"

Lissa leaned against a branch and stared up through the vines. "Think. Think," she murmured fiercely. "Those pioneers found ways. Nimrod and Mellissa and..."

Crick whacked his forehead in disgust. "Forget that! Think about *us. Now.*" He broke a twig in half, then another and another. "Pan's been so quiet lately. He's been hiding under the plant near the wall, just sitting and listening. He thinks he can hear better; learn the giants' plans." He began stringing the twigs together with a length of vine. Ripple watched curiously. Crick could think of more ways to use sticks and dirt and grass. "But what good is listening going to do? We need action!" he cried, and threw his twig bundle down.

Ripple held up her hand as a sound—no, a feeling—came to her. "Quiet." She tensed. "Can you hear it? Feel it?"

At the same moment Pan pushed aside the vines and burst into their shelter. "Giants are surrounding the forest," he said grimly. "I heard them say they will do something with their tools in here. We must take deep shelter!"

They stared back at him, stunned.

"Take the vine paths," Pan ordered, giving Crick a shove. Ripple and Lissa followed across the forest, which trembled with the giants' noises and movements. The memory of the huge staring eyes came back to Ripple. Hundreds of such eyes could be peering right now through the glass, trying to find them as they stumbled toward the tunnel under sheltering vines.

Mother's face filled with relief when she saw them approaching. But her voice was angry, sharp. "Get below. Hurry."

Voices shouted in through the sky dome hole. Vibrations shook the forest.

And then it came, just before they reached the shelter and tunnel. Ripple was the first to see the incredibly long stick reach in through the dome hole.

She didn't want to watch. But her eyes were frozen to the terrifying sight, as the stick plunged its long jabbing claw straight down to earth.

XII

The Giants' Claw

The claw raked the earth with a tearing sound. And where the flat dirt had been was now a hilly lump. The stick came down again, this time touching the moss. Ripple thought in panic: they found out that their poison didn't work so now they are

using their claws. Oh, why couldn't they have waited a few seconds more, so we could have reached the safety of the tunnel? This flimsy vine shelter was much too close to that monstrous claw.

"It's getting closer!" Lissa's gray eyes were enormous in her thin face. Ripple backed away slowly on her stomach, while her eyes followed the long-armed claw.

Crick stood rigid, watching. "What is it going to do?"

No one could answer. They could only watch the claw scrape jerkily across the dirt, leaving a scarred path behind. Slowly it pawed its way down the slope and sunk its claws right into the web-covered eating plant.

"Our food bush!" And Mother clapped her hands over her mouth in horror.

"It's attacking it!"

The claw withdrew, bringing several tangled strands of stems and leaves back with it. Uncle Kane moaned as if the claw had torn into him. "The end," he croaked. "Even the magic cannot save us now."

Pan crouched beside Lissa. His eyes never moved from the claw; his face was set in a grim, hard look.

Again the claw jabbed into the ailing food plant. This time it struck deeply, snaring its prongs into the very heart of the plant. And when it withdrew, the entire plant came away with it, with a great tearing of roots and dirt. Only a large hole in the dirt remained.

By instinct, the six in the vine shelter moved closer together. The claw slowly raised itself above the forest, with the plant dangling in its grip. Higher, higher, it rose, trailing long naked roots, like tails below it.

The sky dome hole was plugged with green leaves. Dirt sprayed from the sky. The next moment, the hole was open, the plant was gone. One long hairy root fell back to earth, broken.

The unthinkable had happened. But before anyone could speak or move, another long stick plunged from the sky. This one had a small stump attached to it. It dropped to the place where the eating plant had been and began thumping the earth. It smoothed and firmed the dirt. A few moments later, no one would have guessed that a plant had ever been there.

Ripple stared, stricken. The power of these giants was beyond all imagining. Not only could they take away weather, wind, and water, they could also make plants appear or disappear at will. They had poison, claws, and that earth-stomping tool.

How silly it had been to think that they could ever escape. They were totally under the giants' great power. And now they had no food. No food. She sank down to the ground, pressing her face against the soft moss. This time Uncle was right.

This time it was surely the end. Whatever hope there had been before, there was none at all now.

Mother slumped against the vine, looking suddenly older. "We've got—to plan," she started, then shook her head. The life had left her voice.

Pan was as still and silent as the bird statue. Grim. Unsmiling. Crick's fingers were clenched around a dirt clod, squeezing it into dust. Lissa's eyes were brimming over.

Clang. Clang. Clang. Clang. Clang. The noise usually only sounded once and then stopped. But this time it kept clanging insistently. *Clang. Clang. Clang.* And then the usual giant noises followed as the great creatures stampeded from their land. Abrupt, sudden, welcome silence followed.

Silence. No more giant faces peering through the glass. No vibrations to shake the ground. Only the long, menacing stick that still reached down to the forest floor.

Ripple gulped. "What . . . what happened? Have they all gone?"

Crick gave her a peculiar look. Then he was out of the vines, running swiftly to the long stick.

"Crick, come back!" Ripple and Mother cried together.

"That's the giants' weapon. Don't touch it!" Lissa yelled. Crick paid no attention. Instead he strode right up to the stick. He looked up where it reached through the sky dome hole. An alarming tingle coursed through Ripple. He wasn't thinking—

"Pan! All of you. Come!" he cried.

Before Crick even finished speaking, Pan was out of the vine shelter. Then Lissa. Ripple followed, wanting, yet not wanting to approach the deadly stick, now still and lifeless. Mother moved even more reluctantly. Uncle stayed in the vines.

"This is it!" Crick cried, stretching his arm out toward the long stick. His eyes snapped. "That must have been some sort of signal. It made them all leave in a hurry. And they left this in!"

"But it is a weapon of the giants," Mother said, eyeing the stick as she would a hairy river creature. "It will surely strike out at us and kill us if we touch it."

"No. It won't kill us." Excitement flooded Pan's voice now, too. "I've lived near these giants all my life. They use tools. This stick is a tool. Doesn't have its own power. It can't hurt us." His gaze swept the full length of the stick. Then he turned and grabbed Crick by the shoulders. "You're right. It's our answer!"

Ripple touched the stick gingerly. "Can we do such a thing?"

"Yes." Lissa grabbed the pole and looked up to the dome hole as if daring it to defy them. "We can." She had cast aside her fear. She stood tall and proud.

Crick's words tumbled out fast. "This is the chance we never thought we'd have. The chance to get out of this evil forest. We can't just stand around and gawk at it. We don't know how much time we've got. Let's start climbing."

He grabbed the pole and took a short, experimental climb, then jumped down. "See?" And he grinned, triumphant. "It didn't strike out at me. It's just a pole. Our escape pole."

Our escape pole. Crick's new way to use a stick. A strange pounding rushed through Ripple's body, from her toes to her head. Pounding excitement. Pounding fear. They could do it.

"But so high," Mother said. "I have been high, of course, in the time of flight. But never like this. Never before the magic."

"Fool idea!" And Ripple spun around at the sound of Uncle's voice, snorting. He stood back from the stick, but his voice called to them sternly. He was the elder again, the advice-giver in a tattered dirty vest. "I am older than the rest of you. I have seen many season cycles: from the spring awakening, to the summer flight time, to the fall days when the wings grow crisp and dry and fall away, to the cold weather when we are burrowed deep in tunnels. Yes, I have seen all these cycles many times, and I know that we have not much longer to wait for the magic. It will save us. Not this." He gazed at the stick with loathing. "This is an instrument of doom. Of doom, I tell you!"

"But our food is gone!" Ripple cried. "We can't wait any longer."

Crick walked over to Uncle. He was shorter than

the old man, but he stood proudly, head thrown back to stare straight into the old storyteller's face.

"We don't have to wait for the magic," he said. "Because the magic has come. This magic." And he pointed to the stick. "Magic or good luck, or whatever you want to call it. Those other stories all happened a long time ago. If this kind of escape is not in those tales, then *we will make our own story.*" He was yelling now. "We will escape!"

XIII

The Escape

Crick's words left a charge in the air. The energy of power and daring. Ripple's eyes followed the stick up to the very top of the forest at the sky dome hole. She could do it. She could climb. She would climb.

Lissa went to Uncle, who was still standing far back from the pole. She took the old storyteller's hand.

"Your songs and stories tell about people who did brave things," she said in her smooth, soft voice. Scarceness of food had made them all thinner. Lissa's eyes took up all the room in her thin face. "Now we have a chance to be brave, too. We must climb."

Uncle looked from Lissa to the long stick. "The magic," he began, like a stubborn child, then stopped and stroked his chin.

"We can't wait any longer," Pan said crisply.

"Let me go first," Crick said, grabbing the pole. He was about to explode with excitement.

"All right. I will stay back to help Uncle. Careful at the top now," Pan warned.

Ripple swallowed hard. As much as she wanted

to escape from the forest, the thought of climbing that long pole brought prickles to her skin. She clenched her fists together tightly as Crick wormed his way up the pole. All the energy that never let him sit still was helping him today. He was agile, quick. In just a short while he had reached the far heights of the bottle.

"Oh, Crick, careful." Lissa shut her eyes, swaying as if she were up there herself. "Hang on tight."

"Fine...fine..." Pan squeezed the word out. His eyes never left Crick. "The boy can climb fine. Hard part will be the slide down. It's steep."

All eyes were glued to the tiny faraway figure climbing out into the giants' world. Crick was so high now, it was hard to tell exactly what he was doing.

"I think he's at the top," Pan said. He gripped the pole and yelled up: "Are you all right?"

A very faint voice floated back down. "Yes. Fine." By squinting hard, Ripple could see him, barely. He was perched right atop the sky dome hole. The sight sent a thrill through her. "He's out! He's out!" she cried.

"Into the giants' world," Mother murmured incredulously. "So high—without flight." She turned to Pan. "But even if we all can get out, what will we do then? We can't go on without some sort of plan—"

Pan's face softened. The crinkle lines almost turned into smiles. "But that's part of the daring, the adventure," he said softly. "Part of the magic, too."

"There he goes!" Lissa almost screamed the words. Ripple's heart plummeted with the tiny figure sliding quick as the wind outside the glassy forest wall. She started toward the glass to see if he survived his breakneck fall. But Pan stopped her.

"We can't lose a moment," he said. "Your turn now." And he lifted her face so she was staring right into those calm blue eyes. "Ready, Ripple?"

Fear grabbed her so suddenly and completely that she was sure Pan could see it leaping out of her eyes or hear the sudden gigantic thumps of her heart. But she wouldn't let her voice show it. She took a step forward.

"Yes. I'm a good . . . climber."

"Be careful, daughter," was all Mother said. But she gripped Ripple's shoulder hard. "We'll be right after you."

Ripple couldn't stop the shudder that passed through her when she stepped on the evil stump to climb the pole. But the others were all standing close, watching and waiting.

Remember the heroes of old, she thought. Remember the scouts, the bravery. There's scout's blood in you. She gripped the pole, wrapping her legs around the wood.

She was a scout now. She was a climber, a pioneer. This is how they would act. Thinking about that made it easier. Move hands. Scoot body up farther. Reach. Slide up more. She made herself look up instead of down. Inch by slow inch she wormed her way up the pole. The tiny dome hole grew closer, bigger. Her arms began to ache. Her legs wanted to relax. But she clung on tightly.

Then, almost at the top, she forgot and looked down. She couldn't see Mother or Pan or Lissa or Uncle. She couldn't find the shelter bush or the slope or the shiny dead bird. The forest spun below her in a green blur. She shut her eyes quickly.

Her hands were clammy. Her legs were cramping. Each push upward took more effort. Crick made it. She could too. She was strong. She was almost there.

She wasn't being a scout. She was being Ripple. The Ripple that had always wanted to explore, even back on the river. The Ripple who wanted to see new places, to have new adventures. She scooted higher.

The sky dome hole yawned closer. She could almost reach it. Panting, she hoisted herself higher on the pole.

The dome hole was still just beyond her reach. Another heave. And then the lip of the bottle was in her slippery grasp, and she was climbing shakily from the pole to the glass rim.

This was surely the top edge of the world. Although she was trembling from the climb and the height, a small triumphant smile touched her lips.

"We will make our own story," she said softly, echoing Crick's words. And then, before the surge of pride left, she turned and lowered herself backwards on the slippery glass dome.

There was no handhold on the smooth glass. She slid slowly at first, then quickly gained momentum as the slope curved over to a sheer drop. Clawing and scrabbling for a handhold, she slid, slipped, and fell the height of the bottle.

I am going to die, she thought in the last split second in midair. Then she hit ground hard, with a jar that knocked the air out of her and set her head spinning.

Crick was right by her side in an instant. "There's some kind of soft stuff on this ground," he said, while Ripple lay still, feeling as if every bone in her body had been rattled loose by the fall. "It hurts—but if that soft stuff wasn't there, the fall could have killed us. I'm sore too."

"How can Mother and Uncle manage that horrible drop?" she asked, when she finally found her voice. "Uncle hurt his leg before. He'll surely break it if he tries this."

"It's not his turn yet," Crick said, pointing up to the bottletop. "That's Lissa up there."

It was a strange, exhilarating feeling to be staring into the forest from the outside. The bottle was huge. She could barely see to the top of it.

But how much time did they have left? When

would the giants return and find them standing unsheltered by the forest? And how would the others make that climb?

"You all right now?" Crick asked.

"Ooh, I'm bruised all over. And my head hurts. But nothing's broken."

"You made it."

"We both did."

They smiled at each other, nervous and proud at the same time.

"I'm glad you're here," Crick said. "It's a scary thing, being the only one out. You did well."

Ripple stared back in surprise. Usually Crick handed out insults, not compliments. "I had to do it. Just like you did." Then, pointing: "Look, Crick, Lissa's ready to start down. And I think that's Mother on the pole, too." Just seeing the two figures climbing gave her stomach a lurch.

A few moments later Lissa slid over the sloping side of the glass and shot down the steep side. Her fall took only a few seconds. Ripple wondered if her own brutal plunge had been so fast. She ran to Lissa.

"Just stay there. Lie back," she said, kneeling beside Lissa, who looked white and stunned. "I felt awful at first, too."

Crick bent down beside her. "You all right, Lis?"

"We're out," she whispered. Her eyes glowed.

"Out of the giants' forest."

Crick leaned back, looking relieved. Right away his tone changed back to bossy brother. "Didn't know you had it in you, Dreamhead."

Mother's turn was next. Ripple could see that she had finished climbing the pole and was already poised on the lip of the bottle. Then she slid down the steep glassy side to land in a heap right beside them.

"Mother, are you all right?" Ripple's breath caught in her throat as she touched her mother's head gently.

A groan answered her. "That fall," Mother said faintly. "That horrible slide, and no wings." Then, "Just give me a minute to catch my breath." She groaned again, shut her eyes.

"Uncle Kane and Pan are going up together," Crick said in a surprised voice. "Looks like Pan is on the bottom. Sort of propping Uncle up."

"Can Pan climb up all the way like that?" Lissa sat up, worried.

"Maybe once Pan gets him going, Uncle Kane can manage part of the climb himself," Ripple said, more hopefully than she felt.

The progress of the two still inside the bottle was agonizingly slow. She watched the two figures inch slowly, slowly up the pole. She thought of Uncle Kane's heavy build, of his age and his fear of the pole—then of Pan's determination and strength. That would have to see them both up the stick. But if Pan should falter, start to loose his grip—begin to slide back under the double weight...

Silently the group watched the climb. Mother forgot her own aches and propped herself up to watch. She murmured, "Pan, you can do it. Keep going. It's not much farther." Then, as the two blurred figures reached the top of the bottle, an ear-splitting clanging noise filled the land. Ripple covered her ears and crouched down in fright. Without the protection of glass walls, the noise was deafening.

"The giants are coming back!" Crick cried, jumping up and down. "Get moving, Pan! They can't find us all like this!"

Frantically Ripple searched for a place to hide. They were standing on some soft material that covered a big area of ground. Not far away were towering wooden structures; on the other side were giant compartments of some sort. They could surely find a safe niche in there somewhere.

"We can hide in there," she said, pointing.

"They're coming down," Lissa said grimly. She held her hand up to her mouth and watched anxiously. Ripple looked too. It was hard to watch old Uncle plummet down the slope with such frightening breakneck speed. Could the old man survive such a slide and fall? As he slumped onto the ground, vibrations shook the earth. The giant noises grew louder. In a short while the giants would be upon them.

Mother took over. "Ripple, Crick, Lissa, pull Uncle Kane over to those compartments. Find a place for us to hide." Fear made her voice shrill. "Hurry!"

They half-pulled, half-carried the moaning old storyteller into a huge compartment. "Now, back for Pan," Ripple said, after they had settled Uncle Kane in a dark corner. She hated to leave Uncle. But there was no time. They would have to wait until everyone was safe, before stopping to take stock of injuries.

"No. Wait. They're already coming." And Lissa pointed to Mother, who was running and pulling a stumbling Pan along with her. They reached the compartment and collapsed beside the children just as the giants surrounded the bottle with a great stomping and much talking.

XIV

The Next Step

As the deafening noise exploded around them, they huddled almost in a heap, out of breath and terrified.

"Foolish venture," Uncle moaned from where he lay. "It will be the end of us all. Ooh, my head."

Lissa knelt beside him. "Is he hurt bad, do you think?"

"He can still use his leg anyway." Ripple was trying to catch her breath. Her legs felt wobbly and her arms ached from pulling Uncle so fast. He was breathing heavily and his face was red. "Thank goodness for the soft stuff on the ground. And he went limp when he fell. That helped." She lowered her voice and pulled Lissa aside. "Do you know what I think? Mostly, he's scared. Just as scared as the rest of us."

Mother was seated by Pan, who was stretched out in the far corner of the compartment. The task of boosting Uncle Kane up the long pole, followed by the fall and the last minute sprint from the giants had sapped every bit of his strength. His grimy headband had fallen off, and his black hair fell in a tangle over his face as he lay, panting hard.

"Just lie there," Mother said for the third time. "Rest. You just did an impossible job."

"No one but Pan could have done it," Crick said proudly. But he looked worried, too. "He'll be all right, won't he?"

Pan grunted a sound that came out between "yea" and "uh." He tried again, turning his head so he faced Crick. "Lost my wind," he muttered.

"Let him rest," Mother said sharply. Crick

backed off, with a surprised glance at Mother.

"Ooh, this bump on my head, and my leg not yet healed..." Uncle spoke in a loud, peevish voice.

Ripple fought a grin. Uncle wanted Mother to stand over him, to tell him to rest, to praise the impossible job *he* had done.

"Ripple, over here." Crick had found a hidden crevice and was watching the giants. "They're everywhere!" Ripple crept over to Crick's spy hole and peered out, fighting back fear.

Crick was right. She couldn't even take in the hugeness of these beings in one glance. They filled the land with color and noise and movement.

"Do you know any of those sounds?" she whispered.

Crick shook his head. "It's all loud noises to me. Pan's the only one who understands what they're saying. He'll tell us about it when he feels like talking."

Ripple glanced back at Pan. "Mother's right. It was impossible, what he did," she whispered.

"The whole thing was impossible. But we did it." The look in Crick's eyes had changed to wonder. "We all did it together."

"Sh—" Pan sat up. He was breathing more normally. "It's time to listen, not talk." And he listened for a long time, until another tremendous clang sent the giants stampeding from their land. The quiet that followed was as welcome and comforting to Ripple as the soft moss at night.

But Pan sat up even straighter. He shook his head as though to clear it; took a deep breath. "Listen, all of you," he began. "They did talk about the bottle prison. They said our eating bush was moldy, whatever that means. They threw it away. But they didn't speak of our escape. I don't think they know."

"It was a good thing we got out," Mother said fervently, and Ripple nodded agreement. In this strange land they were still in giants' territory and still shut out from the wind and river water and warm sun, but at least the heavy, wet air and glass wall were gone.

"Now. Here's the important part. They're taking some sort of trip. Now remember, I grew up near giants. I know some of their talk. But not all of it. I don't understand about this trip. It will be on some creature called Bus. It will go to a place with trees and grass and water."

"Trees . . . grass . . . water," Lissa echoed, making each word sound more wondrous than the one before. "Oh . . ." It was a long, yearning sigh.

Crick sprang up. "We'll go too!"

"No, no," Uncle Kane protested. "We are losing strength. We are bruised, hungry, weak. We are not ready for more dangers. We must wait. Here, out of the bottle, it would be so easy to wait for the magic." There was a pleading note in his voice. "Then we will have freedom to go anywhere."

Crick opened his mouth, but Uncle rushed on. "While you children were climbing the pole, Fern gathered the last of the food leaves. She always plans well. Her pouch is filled with the remaining food leaves. With rations we can wait, wait here in this shelter." He started to slide into his storyteller's tone. "Remember, in the days of—"

"It's the day of *now!*" Ripple cried, then stopped, surprised at her own rude outburst. But Uncle was wrong. They did not dare linger here, in this treacherous land of the giants, and nibble on a few stale leaves while he wove spells of long ago. There was no time to wait for the magic.

Crick clapped his hands. "Well done!" His smile was wide and approving.

"Crick, be quiet!" Pan snapped.

Mother turned to Uncle. "These leaves will not go far. And some are already tinged with the white poison. We dare not wait here. We will starve if we do. Do you see?"

"This is still giants' territory," Pan added. "Not much better than the bottle." He reached into his pouch for a lantan weed, then remembered with a scowl. "Have to get by without them." He turned to Crick, Ripple, Lissa. "That trip's our best hope. Pay attention. If a chance comes . . . we must be ready."

XV

The Chance

It was Ripple who spied the chance. When the giants thundered back into their land, she forced herself to watch them, just as Pan had ordered. She found another crack in the wood where she could safely observe the huge, loathsome beings at a distance. At first, just the sounds and the strange scents sent shudders jumping through her. But she made herself stay. After a while, the shaking quieted. The fear changed to curiosity—and fascination.

The giants' forms are said to be like our own, Mother had once told her. Perhaps it was true. Perhaps those masses of flesh were arms, legs, bodies, and faces. Some of the creatures were very close to her crack. She stared hard at the hugeness, trying to make sense of it. Yes, that was the lower part of a leg, a monster of a leg, sprawled directly outside the compartment. She could see the frightening details of the colored foot cover and the leg coverings that turned up to form a pouch at the bottom.

Somewhere in the back of her mind she heard Pan's voice. "I was trapped. I climbed up that giant's foot. There was material covering it. And there I clung." She stared hard at the giant's leg pouch.

It was a preposterous idea, really. Even if she could bring herself to make a suggestion like that, none of the others would go along with it. It was too dangerous. There had to be a better, safer way. After all, the giants were the enemy. Monsters. Beasts. One didn't jump toward them of one's own free will.

A few minutes later she stood before the rest of the group, telling them about the leg pouch. She didn't have to actually describe the plan. They grasped the idea right away.

"Preposterous! Suicidal!" Uncle Kane cried in horror.

Mother said slowly, "It sounds even worse than the climb from the bottle."

Pan's eyebrows pulled together in a hard-thinking look that came out like a frown. "It's a big risk," he muttered. "Mighty big risk." He glanced at Mother. "But possible. Maybe."

"You have gone mad. All of you," Uncle said in a deadly calm voice. Lissa said nothing, but rose slowly and went to see the great leg and pouch herself. The others joined her, crowding around Ripple's spy hole, staring at the leg.

Then came a sudden burst of noise, a babble of talk. Several giants moved. The leg before them shifted slightly, bumping right against their compartment.

Pan spoke in a very low voice. "This is it. It's now or never. They are going to leave." Then in the same calm voice, "Jump, Ripple."

No more time. Not even a moment to stand and gather courage for such a dangerous leap. But she was getting used to danger. Danger was everywhere today: in the air, in her lungs and her head and her legs. And perhaps it was better that she had no time to really consider the jump. Her wildly banging heart seemed to jump out ahead of her as she tumbled down into the soft, yielding pouch just below.

A moment later Crick jumped in. He sprawled right on top of her. "Diy," he moaned, rubbing his head. "You have a hard head."

"Here comes Lissa. Move!" Ripple gave him a push, as Lissa toppled between them. Next came Mother, landing in a heap beside them.

"Spread out, spread out! We don't want him to feel us in here," Ripple hissed. She bit her lip. He'll know, she thought. He'll know. He'll feel our weight. One of us, two of us, maybe even three of us could get away with it. But six! She should have never brought up this wild scheme. Uncle was right. It was mad.

But the giants' land was filled with movement and sound. No huge hand reached down to grab them, even when Uncle Kane's heavy body sank into the pouch.

Crazy. Crazy. Ripple helped Uncle to move and make room for Pan. Part of her mind was floating above her, watching incredulously and saying, "Can this really be happening? Are we really all jumping like madmen into the giants' clutches? Am I really doing all this?"

"No one move unless you absolutely have to," came Mother's voice, tense, panicky. Then, "Oh, my. Oh, my," as their pouch lunged forward into the air and came down with a jarring thud. Ripple clutched the leg-covering material to keep her balance. Lurch, *thud*; lurch, *thud*; lurch, *thud*. The leg jerked forward on its journey, carrying them into the great regions of the giants' land.

XVI

The Journey

The creature called Bus made terrible vibrating noises. Crouched in shadows at the bottom of the pouch, Ripple waited for the ordeal to end. She did not try to talk to the others. Even if she had dared to move, she could barely have heard their voices over the din.

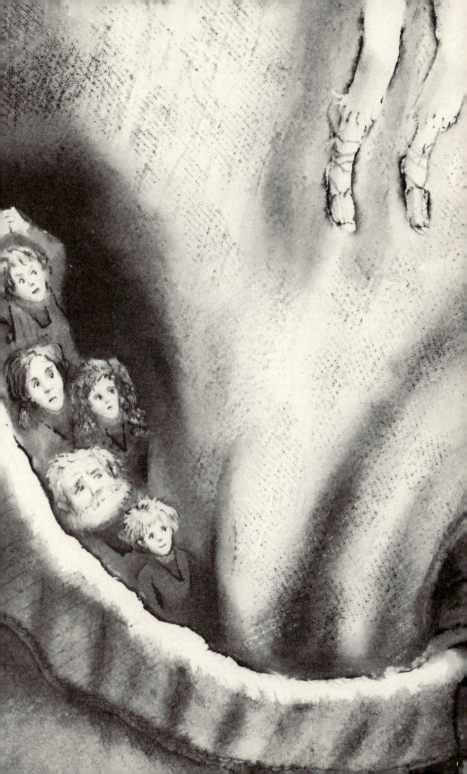

She felt a light punch on her arm and turned to see Crick beside her. He gave her another quick punch. "Do you believe it?" He leaned back against the pouch, stretched, and moved again. Poor Crick, who could never keep still. He looked ready to burst. Even his eyes snapped. "We're doing it, Ripple. We're going!"

Yes, it really was happening. She was tingly-numb, but it was happening. Our own brave story— She turned to Lissa. "Are you all right?" she said loudly, so Lissa could hear. Her own voice sounded shaky.

Lissa's eyes were closed. "Green grass, water, fresh air," she said with determination. She opened her eyes and looked at Ripple. "Think about that. Think about it real hard."

Lissa was smart. She was dreaming herself past this terrible shuddering ride. Ripple shut her eyes and tried it too. Tried to imagine green grass, the feel of wind and sun. But the loud coughs and rumbles of Bus bumped into every blade of grass in her mind. And Uncle's moan cut into her day-dream.

"Oh, what is to become of us? From one prison to another!"

"If we only knew what lay in store at the end of the trip," Mother worried out loud. "Then we could plan . . ."

Bus gave one last rumbling shudder and fell silent. The giants moved again, with more loud noises. Ripple fell backward against Crick, who toppled into Pan, as the foot they were on rose swiftly into the air.

Other legs pressed close, jostling, crowding. Then, with one long, hard thud, the leg stopped. The giants' babblings drifted away in several directions and new noises took their place. Noises that sent tingles of happiness through Ripple.

"Birds!" Lissa said, grabbing Ripple's arm. "Can you hear them? They're all around us. Birds! Real, live, song-making birds!"

"And other flying creatures. The ones that buzz and drone. I can hear them, too," Uncle said incredulously. "I never thought I would hear such sounds again!"

Pan took a long deep breath. A slow smile lit his face. "After the damp rotting air of that forest, this smells wonderful." He drew another breath. "Water. I smell water."

"A river?" Ripple cried.

"No. I don't think it is a river, or we would hear it moving. But there is water. I'm sure of it. Now, if we can manage to escape from this leg pouch and reach some shelter. . . ."

It was a very big if. It brought silence to the group. Ripple gazed at the fabric wall that had hidden and protected them so far. If they could not climb back out at the right time, these walls would become another prison.

Pan stared up at the pouch brim. "We should

have a scout up there. Someone who can see what's going on and give the signal to the rest of us."

"I'll do it!" Crick was practically hopping on one leg in his eagerness. "I'll go."

But Ripple was already climbing, grabbing handholds from the small knobs in the material. She couldn't stay in the bottom of that dark crowded pouch another moment. Not when such wonderful smells and sights and sounds were almost within reach. She was a scout. She could do it. She could watch; give the signal. Handhold by handhold, she pulled herself to the top. Grabbing the rim of the pouch tightly, she peered out in delight at the great outside.

She had forgotten the color of the sky; forgotten its bright blueness and its mounds of soaring white clouds; forgotten even the feel of the wind in her hair. All these sensations rushed over her with such force she almost lost her balance.

"Duck lower," Mother whispered sharply. "You can be seen." As she spoke, their leg shot forward again, with a jerk that almost tumbled Ripple from her post. With a desperate grab, she regained her hold.

"We're crossing the grass area. Lots of giants around. They're running toward something." She stared at the great expanse of blue over the horizon and cried: "Water! There *is* water! You were right, Pan. A huge great lot of water!"

Crick and Lissa both started to climb up, but

Mother called, "One scout's enough. You might be seen. Down."

"Are there plants near the water?" Pan called tensely. "Plants that could hide us?"

"Lots of them. We haven't reached them yet."

"Now, Ripple, watch carefully. When the giant stops close to one of those plants—"

"I'll give the signal," she finished. That tingly, pounding feeling rushed over her in a wave. This was it. The last and perhaps the most dangerous part of the escape. She felt ready to explode with nervousness. She could sense the mood of those in the pouch: tense, anxious, waiting for the signal.

"We'll need two jumping-off places when the time comes," Mother said suddenly. "That way we can all get out faster."

"Good idea," Pan said. "Crick, Lissa, get over there by Ripple's post. I'll stay on this side and help Kane. But everyone should climb near the back of the foot. It's safer." He turned to Mother. "And Fern—"

"I will stay here to help you with Kane," Mother said. There was a note in her voice that made Ripple stare down into the pouch curiously.

But there was no time to wonder at that or at the look passing between Pan and Mother, for suddenly the foot stopped. Ripple's head came up with a jerk. It was time. She knew it at once.

"Now! Start climbing!"

"Diy, let's get going, before he moves again."

And Crick gave Lissa a boost up. "Go down with her, Ripple. I'll come next."

"Don't move, foot, don't move," Lissa hissed fiercely, as she climbed. "Let us all get away before you move."

"It can't move. It *can't*," Ripple said. She grabbed Lissa, pulled her over the edge. "Ready?" For a split second they hung there together. Lissa tossed her hair back and pressed her lips tight.

"We'll make it."

Ripple gulped. "Now!"

They dropped down the outside at the back of the foot and ran toward the nearest plant. Fear whirled around Ripple in dizzy circles. This was worse than the climb from the bottle, worse than the fall, worse than the jump into the pouch. This was the invasion, happening all over again. The crushing stomping giants everywhere and noise and fear. She was sure with every step that a huge foot would crash down on them, or some strange creature from this new land would appear.

By the time she reached one of the sheltering plants, her breath was coming in gasps. She dived under the leaves, with Lissa close behind.

"Never...been...so...scared...in my life," Lissa panted.

"Mother's down. And Uncle. She's bringing him with her." Ripple and Lissa both reached out for them, yanking them into the safety of the plant.

"Climbed down myself," Uncle said, then sank

heavily to the ground. "By the Great Nimrod, I never thought I'd reach this plant."

Next came Pan, running fast and hard.

"Where's Crick?" he asked at once, as he crawled into the shelter. "He should be here by now."

They all turned to look. Ripple's eyes opened wide with horror. The foot that they had just left was moving up into the air, with a small figure clinging to the outside of its leg pouch.

Crick had not jumped down in time.

XVII

Our Own Brave Story

"No," Mother groaned.

"Crick!" Lissa yelled, wild-eyed. Ripple felt sick. This couldn't be happening. Not now, when they were all so close to the end of their long journey.

Pan took a deep breath. His voice swelled louder than Ripple had ever heard it. "Drop, Crick. Run!" But even that mighty effort was lost in the noise of the giants. The foot moved faster, carrying Crick further away from them. They could still see him clinging desperately to the pouch; he would soon be lost in the distance.

Suddenly, they were all moving, too, running along the path's edge, trying to keep him in sight. Even Uncle Kane was trying to hurry. So they all saw Crick fall to the ground and sprawl in the dirt.

Lissa screamed.

"Hurry, get him!" Ripple cried. "Before someone tramples him." The distance that the giant had
covered in a few strides took them forever. But the
giants that had filled the road just a few minutes
before were stomping off into the distance now.
No huge feet descended upon Crick's still form.

Pan reached him first. "Can you get up? Is
anything broken?"

"My foot's hurt. I fell just as the giant's foot

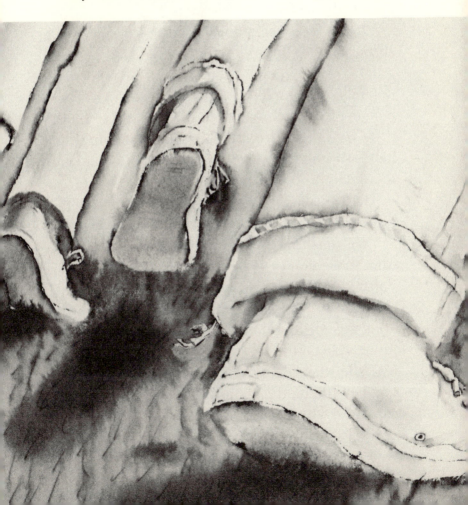

came up. I hit the ground twisted." He tried to move and winced.

"Let's move him. Fast." Mother straightened. "Ripple, take one leg. Lissa, grab the other, above the hurt part. Hurry!"

Pan lifted Crick under his arms. With Ripple and Lissa each carrying a leg, they started back into the underbrush. Mother turned to get Uncle Kane, who was still moving slowly but steadily toward them, favoring his weak leg.

Crick's face was grim. "My foot got caught in a string hanging from the pouch," he said between grunts, as they jounced him along. "I couldn't get untangled. Then the foot started moving. I was hanging by that thread, and when it broke, I fell."

To be hanging by a thread from a stomping giant foot—Ripple exchanged a look with Lissa. Crick was lucky to be alive.

They pushed farther into the foilage. Mother refused to stop under the first good sheltering plant.

"We must get well away from the path, as far from those giants as possible," she insisted. And Pan nodded agreement. So they pressed on, through the underbrush that grew steadily denser. Ripple's arms ached from their burden. And Uncle's hobbling was getting slower and slower. "Ooh, my leg," he wheezed. "Can't go much farther, Fern."

Above them, the plants formed wide, concealing canopies. The air buzzed with life. The water smell grew stronger. And Ripple's burden felt heavier.

"I just can't go any farther." The ache in her arms was becoming unbearable. "If we don't stop, I'll drop Crick's leg."

"Just around this next broad-leafed plant," Mother urged. She was supporting Uncle around the waist now. "We must be far enough from the giants by now."

They rounded the plant and stopped short. They had come to the shore of a wide stretch of water that reached as far as they could see. It did not rush and splash like the river that Ripple had known before. This water lay calm and smooth before them, and it was so clear that they could see sandy pebbles beneath it. Her eyes widened. Where only tiredness had been a moment ago, a strange excitement was growing. "Is it a river?"

Pan shook his head. "No, it's too calm." He set Crick down, then straightened with his hand on his back, legs apart, watching. A slow smile spread over his face. "Water. Real, true water. We made it."

His words and smile were like a spell uncoiling the springs inside all of them, pushing past the aches and the tiredness. Suddenly they moved toward the cool wetness. Smiling. Wading, splashing, even laughing. Everyone except Uncle, who lay on the shore, too tired to move. Even Crick slid over to feel the water and splashed some on Lissa's arm. "We made it, Dreamhead," he said. "Even without the magic."

Ripple watched Lissa splash him back, then lean over and hug him, to everyone's surprise. Crick ducked, grinning. The joy was too great. Ripple had to do something to let it out before it burst inside her. She scooped up a handful of water and threw it at Crick, where he lay back on the shore.

"Wake up, Dreamhead," she mimicked, in her best "Crick" voice. "We made it."

"Out of that dead place, back into life," Lissa said softly, so softly that only Ripple heard her. Yes, those words said it best. Back into life. Back into that wonderful, dangerous web of sights and sounds and smells called life. Back to the wind and sun and rain, and away from that place where only shiny frozen birds could feel at home.

"Ah-ha!" Pan scrambled down to the water's edge and pulled a few weedy stalks from the bank. "Lantan weeds!" He stuck one in his mouth triumphantly. Mother groaned.

"Filthy weeds, and all that spitting—" But her eyes were still smiling. She looked at Ripple. "We are silly with happiness. But there is so much to do— We must build a shelter for us all. We don't know what other creatures stalk this land. Someone must scout out our food supplies."

Plan, keep busy, do our share. Whether on the riverbank, in the bottle prison, or here in this strange land, Mother was still Mother. Organizer. Worker. Planner.

"Tonight?" Crick asked incredulously. "You think anyone can do all that work tonight? I can't even walk. And everyone else is about to drop!"

Pan chewed his weed slowly, savoring every crunch. He turned and aimed the seed into the water, then leaned back with a long sigh. "Best lantan I've ever tasted. And Crick is right. We're too tired for great jobs tonight. Tomorrow."

Ripple smiled, a secret, satisfied smile. She hadn't even had to argue with Mother. The others had done it for her. And their arguments had worked better than hers ever did. For Mother was relaxing against the bush now too, with a soft, warm look that Ripple had not seen for a long, long time.

"It can wait," Mother agreed. "What we need most, I suppose, is rest. We've done so much today."

The water had a soothing sound. It kept them there, sitting and listening until the forest darkened with night shadows. The remote giant sounds that had ruled their lives for so long had completely disappeared. New night noises pierced the air. Ripple felt wrapped in warm air and soft sounds.

Of course there were dangers here. Of course they needed to build a shelter to protect themselves from enemies. But later. Later they could do those things.

Lissa's voice broke the silence. Her voice was low and dramatic. "In the days of Pan and Fern and Kane and the children Crick and Lissa and Ripple, there came a great invasion of giants. And the giants destroyed their homes and captured them and imprisoned them in a silent forest. They put a glass wall around the forest. When the prisoners schemed to get out, the giants put their poison scent into the forest." Her voice grew stronger, surer. She stared dreamily into the water.

"And they raked the ground with their claw. But the prisoners escaped. They turned the evil claw of the giants against them. They braved great dangers and traveled to a far distant land and escaped the giants' power." Her voice dropped. She stared at her audience, and there was power and triumph· in those smoky gray eyes. "And all this they did before the coming of the magic."

There was a moment of surprised silence when she finished. Lissa had made their story sound as brave and wonderful as those long-ago adventures of the first pioneers. This was different than her other dreamy moods and verse-making. With this tale, she seemed almost a different person. Wiser, full of dignity and power.

"Well done," Pan said finally, in a husky voice.

"You can do it just like Uncle Kane!" Crick said admiringly.

"Yes," Mother agreed. "She has learned the way of the storyteller."

But it was Uncle who was the most affected by Lissa's unexpected talent. He hobbled slowly over

to stand beside her. For once he seemed unable to speak. She looked up at him. "We made our own brave story," she said softly.

It took Uncle Kane a while to get his words out. "I will teach you more," he said at last, stumbling over his words. "You need to know it all. You can do it. You have the power! You can weave great story spells, pass on the culture, tell of the heritage of Nimrod and Mellissa. You, Lissa."

Lissa. Mellissa. The names were so much alike. And there sat Lissa, straight and poised and, somehow, beautiful. Perhaps the mother that Lissa had never known had named her for that long-ago heroine. It fitted. Especially tonight, it fitted.

This must be how a Gathering feels, Ripple decided, watching the proud faces around her. My first real Gathering. We are the pioneers, starting a new colony. That long ago Gathering on the river did not seem so important anymore. She did not even feel like the same person who was captured. These were her people now.

Later, as she snuggled into the hollow of the mossy rock shelter Pan had found for them, she was still hearing Lissa's words: "And they did it all before the coming of the magic."

The magic. It would come now. It would find them here. They would have their time of flight. She was old enough. She would soar over the great water, over the surrounding plants.

On the edge of sleep, a new thought nudged at her mind. Those wings. Those wonderful strong wings that would flare out from her back. She had seen them every summer on the older people. They were large. And the little sky dome hole in the bottle had been small, so small that there had barely been room for her to climb out over the pole.

If we had waited for the magic to come first, we would never have escaped, she realized, with a peculiar feeling deep inside her. Those big wings would have made us prisoners forever. They would not have saved us. They would have destroyed us. She had to talk, to share her new thoughts and feelings.

"Crick?"

"Huh, what?" He sounded drowsy-mad at being awakened.

"You were right. The stick was the magic this time. It saved us."

He grunted.

"But Crick, the other magic will come."

Silence.

Lissa's voice joined in. "It will find us here, Crick. It will come."

The others were stirring now, too. Uncle called, "The signs are right. The time is almost here."

Pan's voice spoke out, deep with drowsiness. "Not tonight, friends."

"I can't wait!" Lissa said with longing. And Ripple looked over at Crick. He was sitting up now, fidgeting restlessly with the moss.

"It can come now that we are out of that place. Yes, it can."

Ripple knew what was coming next. She hurried to say it first, but their voices came together, with perfect timing.

"Diy!" And this time it was a cry of triumph and of promise.

PROPERTY OF THE
NORTON PUBLIC LIBRARY.
25176